THE EVIL OF THE DAY

THE EVIL OF THE DAY

by

THOMAS STERLING

"Basta al giorno il male di esso."
—Matteo 6–34

PERENNIAL LIBRARY
Harper & Row, Publishers
New York, Cambridge, Hagerstown, Philadelphia, San Francisco
London, Mexico City, São Paulo, Sydney

A hardcover edition of this book was originally published by Simon & Schuster, Inc. It is here reprinted by arrangement.

 For information address Simon and Schuster, Inc., 1230 Avenue of the Americas, New York, N.Y. 10020. Published simultaneously in Canada by Fitzhenry & Whiteside Limited, Toronto.

First PERENNIAL LIBRARY edition published 1981.

ISBN: 0-06-080529-3

81 82 83 84 85 10 9 8 7 6 5 4 3 2 1

THE EVIL OF THE DAY

CHAPTER ONE

The crowd held back, with the nervous patience of city people, which so much resembles the impatience of others, while the boat drifted toward the platform. The piling shuddered, a bell rang, and the guard opened a section of the railing. A well-ordered mob surged toward the station doors and another of equal size flowed back on the deck. From below, opaque water boiled up like milk, and the boat resumed its drab civil journey, ignoring the monuments to great wealth which lined its route.

Five hundred yards up the canal it drew again into the left shore to exchange passengers; and once more it swerved out, leaving, as it always did, one or two who had been stuck at the change booth or who had walked when they should have run. Within the cabin, women with shopping nets and men with folded newspapers awaited their turns, occasionally glancing toward the shore for familiar landmarks. They were ordinary people; especially here, as all who ride public conveyances have a similar droop to their eyes and a common tightness around the jaw. But one of the men was easily distinguishable from the others. He was clearly not a Venetian and probably not an Italian. He stared with awe at the lacy structures of colored marble along the Grand Canal—rather, he looked at them, a thing the other passengers were unwilling to do. Nor was he a tourist. He carried a small suitcase which obviously had no room for gaily colored shirts and useless white slacks. He was well dressed, which also proved that he was not traveling for pleasure. He was wearing a heavy trench coat, appropriate for a North Italian April; and beneath his dark, serious face a small bow tie sat like a well-behaved bird, which meant that he was either American or French. A look at his shoes proved he wasn't French.

The young man got off at the Rialto and looked carelessly up and down the promenade. He walked to the left, then returned to his starting point and put his bag down. From a rumpled green package he drew a cigarette and lit it slowly. He also touched the right breast of his jacket, revealing where his wallet was and how little it contained. He peeked at his watch. It was nearing one o'clock and the invisible sun had churned a cloudy sky to a warm grey. Behind him the water of the canal chopped gently, as though recovering from a storm or preparing for one. A new wave of passengers poured from the station. Picking up his bag he went resolutely to the right and stopped at a side wharf. He approached a gondolier. The man's gaily banded straw hat was pushed back on his head and he was reading a comic book.

"*Dov'è quest'indirizzo, per favore?*" the young man said, in a confident but thick accent. He pulled a piece of paper from the left-hand pocket of his jacket.

The gondolier glanced at it. "You want to go? I can take you."

The young man paused, too preoccupied to realize that he was being addressed in his own language. Again he touched his breast. "How much will you charge?" he said, this time in English.

The gondolier seemed disappointed. "I spent twelve years in America," he said. "New York."

"Yes?"

"I worked in the park department."

"How much will you charge?"

"All them boats up at the lake. You know, Central Park?"

"Yes, I know. What's your fare?"

The man shrugged, a bit too quickly. "Not much. Come on, get in." He looked down at the bobbing black beak of his gondola.

"But *how* much?"

He sighed and glanced at the ruffled waters of the canal. "It's a long way. Lot of turns, too. Back in the city it's not the same as out here in the canal. You need . . ."

"Yes?"

He turned suddenly. "Oh—I'd say a couple of thousand lire."

The young man shook his head. "I can only spend six hundred."

The gondolier stared at him thoughtfully "Make it a thousand, O.K.?"

"Six hundred is all I can spend."

Again the man looked out toward the water, rolling and unrolling the comic book with nervous brown fingers. Then he turned back. The faint nod he gave was a bow to the off-season. He picked up his single long oar and jumped to the waiting gondola. The young man followed him down mossy stairs to the water. He stepped lightly into the cockpit, which boasted a red carpet, and took his place on the cushioned bench in the rear, facing the high prow.

"Didn't you like it in New York?"

"I liked it O.K. but I inherited this gondola. They come down in the family." He shoved out from the wall and expertly fluttered the oar in the widening space of water. "It's not just the boat. It's a valuable property if you want to look at it that way, but there's more than that."

"I suppose there is."

"It's a steady living. And when I get old I can always apprentice one of my nephews and take it easy."

They turned in a wide circle. "I hope that will be a long time from now," the young man said, politely. "Maybe the boat will break down before."

"No, they last a long time. That's what's good about it. It's not bad growing old if you got something somebody else can inherit. You get treated right."

"I see."

"When a man dies he needs money. That's what it's for, don't let anybody kid you." As they moved slowly into the side canal the black boat looked like a floating catafalque.

"*C'è Signor Fox?*" He stepped back from the doorway.

"*Chi lo desidera?*" the butler answered.

"Mr. Fieramosca. William Fieramosca."

"*Guglielmo?*"

"No—William."

The young man's voice carried well in spite of its softness. He stood on a marble banistered landing. Behind him the gondola drifted away; its owner was seated on the back deck sipping an orange soda. Above, at the left side of the great house, a delicate marble bridge connected it with a walled garden on the opposite side of the canal.

The butler, whose mournful manner was enlivened by his striped cotton jacket and rabbity white gloves, looked at the young man's suitcase. Mr. Fieramosca placed it in his hand. He stood aside.

"*S'accomodi.*"

"*Grazie.*" He walked through a narrow hall which led to an enormous room tattooed from the floor up with pointless decoration. The butler put down the suitcase and disappeared through a door which lurked among some painted foliage. At the far end of the room, in the right-hand corner, a graceful staircase led to the upper floors. But in the left-hand corner, another staircase was drawn on the wall in perfect perspective—identical to the first in all respects but the important one. There were also chairs painted along the sides of the room which were cruelly like several real chairs standing beside them. A window through which no air had ever passed framed a view of the bridge over the canal. Beneath it, on water which could not flow, rested a gondola. The painted people sitting in it were dressed for an afternoon two hundred years ago. And within the room were several false Venetian mirrors reflecting the faces of people long dead.

The butler re-entered and held the door open. "*S'accomodi, signore,*" he said, his manner stiff with respect.

William passed into a long carpeted hall. At the end of it he came to a small, self-service elevator, thickly painted with tiny flowers. He entered and turned to ask the floor, but the butler firmly pushed in behind him, closed the doors, and snapped the mother-of-pearl button marked "1" with a gesture of defiance to all self-service devices.

The machine rose with patrician languor for one story. The butler led the way and William stepped into a dim hallway nearly the width of a room. Along one side hung a group of eighteenth century portraits of men whose weapons could have been rocket guns instead of rapiers, so little did they resemble anyone now alive. The walls were clothed in deep gold velvet. They walked toward a double paneled door at the end of the hall. The young man's heels clicked shamefully on the marble floor. His guide stopped, pounded twice on the left panel with the butt of his fist and threw his weight against it. The door drifted open and William entered.

"How are you, sir!" a voice boomed.

He looked toward one of the windows, behind which the shutters were half drawn, letting in the room's only light. Then he turned slowly to the left, until he located the chair from which the deep voice had come.

"Very well, Mr. Fox. I believe you are Mr. Fox?"

"I am."

"I didn't bother to wire. I hope you expected me today."

"You were very prompt. Would you like more light?"

"Yes sir."

"I have no objection." The old man glanced toward the window.

William went to the tented shutters and opened them. The window gave on the canal. When he turned back he saw that he was in a large studio, lined on two walls with books but furnished for comfort, not study. Mr. Fox's chair was placed in the middle of the room. There was a smaller one beside it. "Is that too much?" the young man said.

"No. I don't like the dark."

William smiled politely and came back to the center of the room. "There are two kinds."

"Of darkness?"

"Yes sir. One which hides you and one which hides someone else."

The old man prodded the other chair with the tip of his toe and William sat down. "I left it that way on purpose. A man shows up better when he's uncertain."

"I know, Mr. Fox. Therefore, I'm afraid I wasn't."

"I see."

"But . . ."

"Yes?"

"One other thing makes me very uncertain."

"Damn glad of it."

"The reason you asked me to come."

The old man laughed as though he enjoyed being thought hearty. "Suppose you tell me why you wanted to come, first."

William's face tightened. "I need—to work."

"You're broke?"

"I . . ."

"Oh, come off it. Poor men are always saying they want work. They really want *money*—isn't that true?"

"Very well. I'm broke."

"And I advertised for a secretary."

William hesitated. "You've read my qualifications, sir?"

"I know them by heart." Mr. Fox pushed himself out of his chair. He had the muscular body of a man who plays squash to lose weight—unsuccessfully. "Cigar?" He went to a large walnut desk and took up a silver box, heavily encrusted with allegorical figures in high relief.

"No thank you." William also got up. "I'll smoke a cigarette if you don't mind."

"I do mind. I don't like my house stunk up with cheap

tobacco. Smoke a cigar, boy. If you're going to stay here you have to learn to live well."

William took one. "That's the point. I don't *know* if I'm going to stay here."

"You won't, if you keep on."

"All right, Mr. Fox. Do *you* think I'll make a good secretary?"

The old man snorted and sank back in his chair. "Hell no! You can't take shorthand, you can hardly type, and you probably can't add."

"I *can* add."

"You want a drink?"

"Yes."

William followed the pointing cigar to a long table presided over by a blackamoor fashioned of Venetian glass. He poured two shots of bourbon, dropped chunks of ice into them and brought them back.

Mr. Fox took his glass and grunted. "Now it's your turn. When you saw my ad in Rome what made you think you had a chance? Why'd you write? At least why'd you tell the truth?"

"About my 'experience' as a secretary?"

"Yes."

"Because you don't offer two hundred dollars a week and board to a secretary."

The old man grinned through a cloud of smoke. "Your salary's three."

William paused and looked up at a Simonetti battle painting above the fireplace. "I thought there was something more. It only cost me a stamp to write."

"That was very wise."

The young man looked at the lengthening ash of his cigar. "But now that I'm here I'd like to be sure . . ."

Mr. Fox waved his hand disdainfully. "You'd like to be sure of the three hundred a week. Failing that you'd like to stall around until you got the first week's salary. Isn't that true?"

"I don't have to earn money by stalling around, Mr. Fox." The corners of the young man's mouth had grown white.

"You have to earn it any way you can. Don't look so blessed noble." The old man emptied his glass and grinned.

Following him, William sipped his drink twice, as though he did not expect to taste good bourbon again for a long while. "I reserve the right to take this job or refuse it, sir. Even if you offer twice the salary."

"Don't get your hopes up. I won't."

"I would like to know—now—what my job really is, or . . ."

Mr. Fox beamed. "Everything in its season, boy." He held out his glass. "Sweeten this. Would you like lunch?"

There was a long pause. Then the word "lunch" had its effect. "I would." The young man took his employer's glass and returned to the blackamoor.

"Press his left eye."

"What?"

"There!" He pointed to the glass figure. "The left eye's for Massimo. The other's for the lights in the hall."

William gingerly touched the glistening eyeball. He filled both drinks and brought them back.

"How'd you land broke in Rome?"

He watched the clouds of silver smoke rise toward the gilt ceiling. "The company was playing to thin houses. Someone had to go and you don't need a stage manager when you have enough girls in G-strings."

"What were you doing with a European company?"

"Teaching them how to put on an American variety show, I suppose." William fingered an ivory chess set on a small table beside him. "Lots of the girls were Americans, too."

"Then you didn't act?"

"No—not here."

There were two heavy knocks and the butler entered. "*Si signore.*"

Mr. Fox asked him to serve lunch when it was ready. Massimo left, and he drew heavily on his cigar. "Not here?"

"I did quite a bit of acting in the States, as I wrote you. In fact, I came here to do a picture, but it fell through. Then I talked myself into the job of stage manager. I can do a little of everything."

"Excellent."

William got up and went to a silver and green tapestry which nearly covered one wall. He passed his fingers over the surface lovingly, then turned. "You still haven't told me why you picked me."

"Hummmm."

"Was it an actor you wanted? You could have said so."

Mr. Fox dropped his cigar in his drink and trusted the glass to the Bokhara rug beneath his chair. "I wanted a flock of letters. Anyone and everyone. It might interest you to know that I got six hundred. I finally narrowed the field to you and an out-of-work airline pilot who had once been a bookie. I chose you."

"But why?"

"Certainly not for your patience, boy. If you're going to enjoy life the first thing you have to learn is to wait. Not too long—just long enough."

"And how am I supposed to know when is 'long enough?' "

Mr. Fox chuckled. "When time's ripe. Everything needs a build-up. Take food. Do you like food?"

"I eat it." William swallowed hard.

"That's not the same. Now take . . ." He had raised his right hand, fingers gathered together like the petals of an artichoke. William smiled at the gesture. The old man nodded. "You see, I've been in Italy a long time."

"Yes, I see."

"There's an old saying: *Inglese Italianato—diavolo incarnato;* 'An Englishman Italianized is the devil incarnate.' Your case is different. You're Italian, aren't you? Or your family was."

"My father, yes. My mother's name was Jones. I suppose there's a proverb for that, also."

"I don't remember any. What'd your father do?"

"He was a gambler in Reno. My mother was a divorce judge's daughter."

The gold clock on the wall struck twice. "That made it a sort of temporary arrangement, didn't it?" the old man said.

"On the contrary, they have lived there happily for the last thirty years. They once had a fight and my grandfather offered them a divorce but my father kicked him out of the house and wouldn't speak to him for a month."

"And the gambling. That went well, too?"

"My father quit before the big money started coming into the town. He didn't like to work nights. Anyway, he had enough then to live decently."

"I see. Tell me something."

"Am I still supposed to be practicing patience?"

For an instant the sun escaped its mask of clouds and glowed on the red and green leather spines of Mr. Fox's books. "For a few moments, yes. I want your opinion."

"Yes?"

"What do you think of this—all of it." His gesture encompassed the study and the house around it.

"Why—it's very beautiful."

"Beautiful, hell! That's not what you're thinking. Come out with it—straight."

William came back to his chair. "All right. I'd like to own it."

The old man shook with a spasm of laughter. "Good! But *what* do you want to own?"

"I don't know—just this." The young man's foot barely scuffed the rich rug. The brown liquid in the abandoned glass tossed.

"Shall I tell you?" Mr. Fox leaned forward. "Shall I tell you what you want?"

"If you wish."

"Money. Not *some* money—lots of it."

"I would have said some."

"That's a sniveling lie." The old man grinned evilly.

William's eyes grew bright. "I don't want three hundred dollars a week as badly as that." He put down the drink and began to get up.

Mr. Fox reached forward and grasped his knee. "Don't take it personally. I mean the statement is sniveling, not you. And I assume you objected to *that* word, not the other. If not, I'm afraid we won't work well together."

"I'm beginning to wonder about that, too. You better tell me what it is you want. I can always catch a train back this afternoon." He paused. "You owe me the fare —second class."

"Good Lord, keep calm, boy. You're young. You can't help the ideas you pick up. What I mean is, you can't even get a rag for your nose without money. The whole world is run on it. People are afraid to admit it because then they'd have to admit they don't have enough. So they pretend money isn't everything and that they just want a little of it to keep body and soul together—until they get it. Then they want a little more and a little more. I call that sniveling, don't you?"

"Sniveling, perhaps. But not necessarily true."

Mr. Fox cleared his throat, got up, went to the window, and spit into the canal. "Nothing is necessarily true," he said, turning back to his secretary. "What I said merely tends to be. That's enough."

"For you."

"Very well, for me. Don't worry, boy. I don't sit in an attic counting dirty gold. I assure you, no pinchpenny ever knew anything about pennies. You have to spend them to know. And now I'll tell you something . . ." He paused for effect. William watched him intently from across the room. "There once existed a race of men. Rich men. They knew about money as no one in the world has ever known. They built this city!" He turned and waved majestically to the purple and rust roofs. "Built it of gold and silver. Do you know what that means? Dollars, pounds, lire, francs, rubles, florins, ducats, scudi, sovereigns, Standard Oil preferred—whatever you name it . . ." He drew a deep breath. "It's all the same. They built this city out of money and lived in it for centuries—spending, spending, spending. No one's ever dared it before or since, boy. One person, yes—but a whole city! Look around you. Look at it!"

Instead William glanced up at the huge chandelier,

shimmering like a nest of diamond snakes in the milky afternoon light.

The old man turned from the window and came back to the center of the room. "I'll admit it. There *were* a few things they couldn't buy. Sunsets are free. So are some flowers. But everything that could be wrapped up and shipped home they bought. They even paid for the water in their canals and the earth they walked on. And they constructed everything you see—every sliver and stone of it. What's more, it's beautiful."

William shook his head. "Then that itself is something you can't always buy."

"You're wrong. This isn't ordinary beauty. It's money-beauty. Twenty-five years ago I came here and I've never left the city since, or tired of it for a minute. Do you think I'd stay that long with a waterfall? Or a God damn daisy? I don't mind beauty, boy. Not at all—but it's got to cost a lot. Well, *this* has . . ." He raised his head and glared about the room. "Fortunately I was rich. Good Lord, how I hate the snivelers who call themselves 'well off.' Those old boys didn't, you can be sure of that. But they're all dead, now. There's nobody like them in Venice any more. The city they built is falling to pieces, but what they left is enough for me. Oh, it even smells of money—tastes of it!"

The old man's face was the color of one of his free sunsets.

"I didn't know money smelled, sir."

"Well it does. Lord, I'm getting hungry." He looked fretfully at the mantel clock and came back to his chair.

"There's one thing you haven't mentioned, Mr. Fox."

"Yes, what? Drink up, lunch will be ready in a minute."

"Friends . . . do you have any?"

There was a long silence. Then William saw that his employer's shoulders were shaking uncontrollably. The laugh started as a high giggle and roared down into bass like a cataract. The young man waited. By comparison his expression was almost prim.

"You see, boy? Patience. Didn't I tell you? Let it get ripe."

"I'm sorry—I don't . . ."

"Time. Ready to drop in your hands. You wanted to know . . ." The laughter subsided into a contented rumble.

"Does that mean I'm about to learn what my job is?" His voice was edged with irritation.

"Exactly. What was it you asked me?"

"I asked if you had any friends."

Mr. Fox nodded. "But you were sidestepping, as usual. You really wanted to know if I could *buy* any, didn't you?"

"I suppose that would follow," William said, dryly.

"Don't try to look disapproving. Your face wasn't built for it. Tell the truth. You'd like to see me do it, wouldn't you?"

"I'd like to see if you *could* do it."

"There's the spirit! A man can't do a job well without enthusiasm."

"I'm sure that enthusiasm would grow if I knew what the job was." His voice had grown surprisingly hard.

"And you shall, my boy. You certainly shall! Patience has its just reward."

But Mr. Fox's own patience was rewarded first. The butler announced lunch. William Fieramosca was forced to concentrate on good food. He did not learn what his work was to be until they returned to the study for coffee.

CHAPTER TWO

In New York, the following Thursday morning, Anson Sims arose from the brass bedstead which had mothered his dreams since he was a boy and pattered naked across marble floors, through an abandoned music room, to a ruined conservatory. He turned on a fountain which was originally meant to fill a small pond surrounded by exotic plants, and to provide the music of water falling on water. But the plants had long since died, the pool was empty, and the water which dripped from a stone dolphin's mouth rapidly disappeared down a drain. Taking a piece of brown laundry soap from the cement ledge, Anson stepped into the basin and resolutely submitted to the cold shower. He scrubbed his timid white body as though he were his own brutal nurse. Then he dried himself on a rough towel and shaved his lean cheeks with the razor his father had given him on his thirteenth birthday—fifty-three years ago.

Back in his bedroom he gave fifteen minutes to his Bible. Although he had been doing this for nearly half a century he had never yet read the book through. The Bible for Anson, as nearly everything else in his life, was made of scraps. He could not think of it as a whole. It was always in pieces to be quoted, fondled, collected—but never blended together. For example, it satisfied a maidenly instinct of his to read the exhortation of II Kings, ". . . Set thy house in order . . . ;" and he never bothered to pass the semicolon to read: ". . . for thou shalt die, and not live."

When he finished this morning's reading he chose a fresh blue suit. It was not in any way different from the one he had worn for the past week, except that it was sponged and well pressed. His other eight suits were identical. Five had never been worn. By alternating the first five, one each week, none of them had to face more than eleven weeks a year. He counted on the present series for another four years. Then, if all went well, the others would last the rest of his life. His ten blue knit ties were imperishable.

Fifteen minutes later he arrived in the main dining room. Paul stood beside the only chair at the long table, guarding a boiled egg and a plate of toast.

"Good morning, Paul."

"Good morning, sir."

Anson sat down and, chidingly, reversed his egg's position in the cup. With the bottom of his spoon he cracked an area the size of a quarter in the large end and carefully peeled away the shell. He ate slowly, dipping toast. Paul placed some letters against the jar of soluble coffee and left.

When he had finished the egg, Anson prepared a little coffee and sorted his mail. He tossed aside a bank statement but carefully studied a grocer's bill. Having been brought up with money he was not as interested in dollars as in cents. He frowned. The figure seemed implausibly high. Food expenses were all the more alarming because they were inexorable. Eating was the ultimate necessity and it was at this point that one's pretense of dominating money was most hollow. He read two fund-raising letters and initialed them at the bottom for one dollar checks. At last he came to a cream-colored envelope marked, "personal." It bore a crest on the back flap and was postmarked Venice. Anson held it loosely and warmed his cup with more water. He felt uneasy. The envelope was far too—voluptuous. He knew no one in Venice. His finger passed slowly beneath the gummed edge and he drew out a matching sheet, folded once.

Old Friend:

When I remember the splendid plans we made together I cannot believe that mine could have come to such a miserable end in the worn-out body of an old man. And yet I must believe it, for I have known for some time that my life was about to close. A few more weeks—a month at the most—is all that I can hope for. I do not know whether to count it among the least or the greatest of my misfortunes that I have no family. A poor man may die peacefully, surrounded by relatives; but a man of means may have no such simple comforts. Too often his last hours are tortured by the unequal distribution he must make of his all too extensive property. It is perhaps a blessing, therefore, that neither my blood nor my name is shared by another living person.

One would give much for the warm hand of a friend during these last days—a cordial hand from the past. It is for this reason that I write. Perhaps I am presuming too much on your charity, but if it is at all possible I beg you to come to visit me before the end. If not—and I shall not blame you for refusing—I pray that you will find time to write me one letter. For the sake of times past I await your reply.

Fondly,
Cecil Fox.

Anson lowered the trembling letter. The most astonishing thing was that he *did* remember Cecil Fox. Vaguely, miraculously, across a chasm of fifty years he saw the exuberant and faintly unpleasant face of a boy in prep school who had been known as "Foxy." For one term they had shared a room. Beyond that shred of information and his own feeling of having been repelled by the boy's misused vitality, he could remember nothing but the reputation he'd had for being enormously wealthy. Anson reread the letter. How was one to know the impression one left on others? An understanding word, a helping hand—anything at all might leave a lasting mark. Clearly he had come to symbolize something in Cecil Fox's life. One had only to imagine what that life must have been. His lips shaped the word, "profligate." Yet he would not reproach the miserable man. He prepared himself a little more coffee.

When Paul returned he found Mr. Anson still at table, which was surprising enough, as his employer's habits were usually predictable to the second. But a greater surprise followed.

"What is the fare to Europe, Paul?"

"Europe, sir?"

"Yes, to Italy. Venice."

"I—I believe several hundred dollars."

"I mean third class," Anson said, impatiently.

"Yes sir."

There was a significant pause. "And by airplane?"

"Even more, sir." Paul began to collect the plates, assuming that the subject was to be dropped.

Anson stood up. He folded the letter and put it in his breast pocket. "I shall be gone several weeks. Not longer than a month, in any case."

"But—unless you go by air—"

"I *am* going by air. When you finish the ironing this morning take a bus to Cartier's and pick me out a man's watch. It doesn't matter what style, but it has to be a very good one."

Paul brushed the morning's crumbs into his tray. He wet his lips before he spoke. "What price range, Mr. Anson?"

"Money is not a consideration. It's for an old friend."

When he had gone, Paul turned to a large painting over the sideboard. It was a portrait of Anson's father, a full-bodied, vigorous man wearing a comfortably upholstered vest and a cutaway coat. It had the quality, common to many protraits of that era, of being merely godlike. At last Paul raised his tray and hurried to the pantry. A phrase had been used in this house which hadn't been heard since the old man died thirty years ago and money, for the first time, had become a consideration.

On Wednesday of that week, in London, Henry Voltor stopped at the Cinema Club for his afternoon glass of sherry. The club had a limited membership and miserable quarters. It had nothing to do with the cinema. The name had been given to the rooms by a previous group who had enjoyed seeing educational films there, and the present membership felt the title so vulgarly inappropriate that it was kept. Henry used the Cinema Club as his mailing address, chiefly for the pleasure of repeating the name to people who had never heard it. For the same reason he insisted that he be addressed as *Mr.* Henry Voltor, and wore the ancient arms of his family on a two-shilling ring which stained his finger green. That protected him from the masses of people who had "taste."

He stopped at the desk for mail and went into the dingy bar where an American juke box—with phonograph records extracted—was flashing horrible pastels, "for the agony," one of the members had explained. The machine was a great success. Henry chose a chair in the far corner, nodding to the waiter.

He looked casually through his mail. He was a solicitor, having diffidently joined the bar in his youth, "to get a trade." He had barely opened a law book since, and had no practice whatever, but he enjoyed keeping an office and going about the city as though he were on business. It had taken him twenty years to get his dispatch case properly scuffed. His profession also brought him more mail than he would customarily receive. He was grateful even for the advertisements. His social life was such that he was necessarily lonely. Henry's few friends blazed like stars on the distant world. But, like stars, they were noticed less than the common moon and the upstart planets. He examined a heavy envelope which lay at the bottom of his little bundle, wondering who could be writing him from Venice at this time of year.

"Your sherry, sir."

Henry looked up wearily, frowning in imitation of a man whose work is never done. "Thank you, Phillip."

"Busy day, Mr. Voltor?" Phillip's voice gently brushed the hidden title.

"Not very," he said, with restraint.

The waiter retired quietly and Henry sipped his sherry. He loved it for its lonely taste, and yet, occasionally, he longed for something more—convivial. But the world was so cruelly arranged that he could not be Henry Voltor and be someone else at the same time.

Except . . . There was a way, of course, but he had never had the means to follow it. If he were immensely wealthy he might change personalities like ties. A few millions and, flip! he was off chasing some barbaric continental princess. Or, flip! he was a vulgar tycoon in one of the Americas, with a great ranch at which he gave the most noisome balls of the century. One could have no end of honest amusement with piles of gold. But unfortunately he was not rich. That made no difference here among his own class, but it would make a great deal of difference elsewhere.

He weighed the envelope in his hand. Venice. The people he knew traveled very little any more. One encountered so many "smart" persons out there. It was their snobbery that was embarrassing. They went about it so crudely. He ripped open the flap and threw the envelope on the table beside his chair. From the first words on the folded sheet he knew that he was being addressed by an American. It was like being clapped on the back (which he loathed). "Old Friend . . ."

When he finished he lay his head back and closed his eyes. He had met a certain Cecil Fox long ago, though that now seemed incredible. There had been a young woman . . . a locomotive manufacturer's daughter. Fairly well brought up. At least not all covered with soot. He and this Fox had been in love with her. Love, in those days, was a leveler and one got to know many people one wouldn't see otherwise. Then the girl married some coal mines (to run her father's locomotives) and in their sorrow he and Fox had become, momentarily, friends. From that miserable beginning had come this. This! Henry's mind was overborne by feverish dreams.

He saw himself as a sinister financier in—Athens? As a heavy-lidded gambler in Marrakech? How delightfully ridiculous. Of course he would have to play his parts well—follow the social customs of the tribes. In Athens he would pretend that money was important; in Marrakech, that it wasn't. What an excellent game. The joys of being a social climber! He might even take a flat in Chelsea and pretend to be something artistic or political. For the secret of society was that no class looked down nor up any further than it had to. With money one could play it like a harp.

He decided to go to Venice. But first he would need bait—more cash than he could lay hands on by himself. He stood up and looked around for Keith Whitestump. He was in his usual corner by the window, at his solitaire. Stumpy's huge fortune had almost cost him a bid for membership, in spite of nearly perfect connections. The "nearly" explained the fortune. He was eager to show gratitude. In any case it was never difficult to borrow from a member. One could have bad debts anywhere in the world but here. A man might lose his membership, and money, after all, wasn't that important.

"I hope you have your checkbook, Stumpy. I need a loan."

The player refused to look up. He held his last card in trembling fingers. With his free hand he reached into his pocket and drew out pen and checkbook. "How much," he said, distantly.

"A pot full." Henry pointed to a red queen on a red jack.

The young man let out his breath in a rush. He leaned back in his chair. "I'm glad in a way. It's rotten to be one off and stuck. Two's not so bad. How much?"

"Five thousand pounds. Back in a month at the usual grinding interest."

Stumpy pushed the cards away and opened the checkbook. "A man has to cheat to win this game. Take my advice, don't let yourself get caught by it. I haven't had time for a haircut in a week." He scribbled his name on the check and tore it out.

"I'm thinking of taking up another kind of game," Henry said.

Whitestump handed him the money. "Good idea. I hope you have better luck."

"I'm sure I will."

"The trouble with this one," the young man said, pointing to the scattered cards, "is that you can only play it alone."

"Perhaps that's why it's called solitaire."

"Good Lord! I believe that's true."

CHAPTER THREE

Celia waited for the wake of their motorboat to catch a gondola. It curved out from the stern like a strand of spider's silk in the wind. There! The black shell rocked. There was a line between them now. She wished she could reach down into the water and drag the gondola to her. Then the line moved on toward the marble façades at the canal's edge and they were alone again in the roaring boat.

Mrs. Sheridan was mumbling. ". . . pay him one cent more than we agreed." Celia looked furtively at the driver, hoping he couldn't understand English. The old woman assumed that people she hired for limited services understood nothing but direct commands. It was even difficult for her to *see* inferiors. At a small hotel the same girl might serve their lunch and bring breakfast trays to their rooms, but Mrs. Sheridan was perfectly capable of asking the chambermaid to tell the waitress that they would not be having their meals in the hotel that day. Even her own face, Celia knew, was an indistinct blur to the woman. She was hired as a "companion" —a sort of spiritual chauffeur with whom communication was carried on through a speaking tube.

"Not one penny."

The voice had acquired an imperious note, which

Celia recognized as a warning to make some reply. The reply itself was not as important as the assurance that she was listening. "I'm sure he asked a good price."

"Good!"

"I mean for him."

"These gondoliers charge strangers twice as much as their own people."

Celia looked straight ahead, over their driver's shoulder. She didn't imagine they were called gondoliers—in Cris-crafts. They swerved toward the center of the canal to avoid a garbage barge. A gull circled over the water before a palace with purple balconies. She longed to change places with it, to throw herself on the air and glide past the lacy stone buildings . . . and the gull, sitting stiffly beside old Mrs. Sheridan, listening to never-ending complaints, nodding its beak, earning its pay. She drowned a smile. A drop of water touched her forehead as they slapped into the swirling currents left by the barge.

"He's taking advantage of me and he knows it."

How could he help but know it, if he were? But the woman didn't mean that. She spoke in code. She meant, "I don't intend to tip," as when she said, "the service is frightful in this hotel," and "that man has an insolent look." A voice called across the water . . . like a horn. A ferry grazed a dock on the left and backwatered. It *was* a street. A boulevard with ripples. And something else, something she had recognized from the first moment. A feeling from long ago. . . .

"I don't know who's worse, the Italians or the French."

. . . But long ago there could have been nothing like this city, even in her daydreams. She had not known any body of water larger than the pool in Antelope Park, or old Salt Creek—which wasn't salty. And yet she remembered . . . a graveyard. Monotonous Sundays in uncomfortable patent leather shoes, following her grandmother along aisles of tattered marble. The smell of clipped, damp grass; of daisies and sweet william; old phlox scattered on the mounds and that other dry, kindly odor of death. Those afternoons were never frightening—merely boring—and grandma spoke comfortably of her daughter and son-in-law who had "passed on." But in spite of that, one learned about death. She knew its face as well as her own. It could never completely change its features. Venice was a graveyard with words of mourning cut into its stones. The odor was here. Celia nodded. She did not have to be afraid of an old friend.

"What's the matter, Celia? You haven't forgotten anything, I suppose."

She looked around quickly. "No ma'am. Nothing, I'm sure."

"I hope you're quite sure. Looking at you, *I* wouldn't be. What are you thinking?"

"Just—thinking, Mrs. Sheridan."

"At least you don't pretend you were listening to me."

"I'm sorry. The city's so fascinating."

"A filthy sewer. Let's hope the house is clean, at least."

"I'm sure it will be very nice."

"You seem uncommonly certain of everything today."

The boat made a wide turn to the left and headed up a side channel which smelled of rotting eggs. The old woman and her companion sat in silence, each secure in the knowledge that their connection depended on a small, regular salary.

Celia had been six months with Mrs. Sheridan. Except for the first two weeks in New York, they had spent all of that time traveling through Europe and North Africa—the whole winter season. They should have been the most fascinating months of her life, but she soon learned that a large hotel in Paris is very much like a large hotel anywhere and that once a customer pays more than five dollars for lunch he is served the same food, in the same way, from Marrakech to Lausanne. As she was not likely to live so expensively again she would not have cared if it weren't for the loneliness. She traveled with a woman to whom she had never spoken a single spontaneous word; and her afternoons off were squandered in parks and museums where she discovered she even missed being able to read the signs which were undoubtedly telling her not to feed animals, trespass, smoke, touch, etc. An evening of staring into shops on the *Promenade des Anglais* in Nice was somehow more desperate than it would have been in New York. She imagined other young women would have been more resourceful—and she wasn't at all embarrassed to think in what ways they *might* be—but one had to have an instinct for the world. She did not. The only country she knew how to live in was bounded by herself, and that seemed to be growing smaller the further away she traveled from voices she could understand on the streets and familiar advertising posters. Here, even the skywriting was unintelligible. As with most people who have grown up in solitude and have nearly got used to it, the smallest ties she had with others were vital.

The worst of it was that she did not *feel* anti-social. She was both attractive and healthy—not just attractive *because* she was healthy, either—and she enjoyed company. But because of an accident, which she usually thought of as ridiculous rather than tragic, she had been forced into another sort of life. Returning from a picnic one pleasant spring afternoon, her father and mother had been killed when their car collided with a cow which had strayed on the highway. As a result she had been brought up by her grandmother in a little house on the outskirts of a midwestern town. Not that this was bad in itself, but a seventy-year-old woman is not the best company for an energetic child. By the time she started school her grandmother had become nearly bedridden, so that she'd had to abandon her friends to nurse the old woman. It was not a terribly hard life, as they had a little money from her father's insurance, but it was too quiet. She learned almost nothing of living and too much of dying. When the old woman "passed on" Celia was left in a world she was only prepared to give up. As she was then eighteen she took the rest of her father's money and sent herself to college. She had become her own parent.

After graduation she worked for a year in New York for a bookstore chain (twelve to nine, thirty-two fifty a week, and throbbing feet). Her money was gone, and though she was able to earn her own living and perhaps even to make a career for herself, she felt like a person who has run for miles to arrive, exhausted, at the starting line of a race. When Mrs. Sheridan offered to hire her as a companion—at a token wage—she quickly accepted. The race, she thought excitedly, had begun. But she had merely become, again, an elderly woman's nurse. The only improvement in her position was that this time she was not working for love. She could always leave, if she were willing to brave the world without money. It struck her as curious that Mrs. Sheridan should also think companionship by purchase had its advantages. Of course she had no one else in the world. Even if she had she couldn't be sure of someone's love forever. But fear of poverty was a fairly certain emotion. Whatever the old woman wanted she preferred to buy—if the price was reasonable.

The boat came at last to a widening of the channel. Celia had been fascinated by the reflections of the houses in the water. They were not as magnificent as those along the Grand Canal, but they seemed—almost because of that—to be hoarding luxury for those inside. Then, on the right, she saw a great square building which was joined at the far end, where the canal narrowed again, to a bone-white travertine bridge. On the left, the brick wall of a garden rose straight out of the water and a branch of a mimosa tree trembled above her. The little bridge led into the garden. The house itself was founded on heavy travertine blocks which were stained with moss and algae; it was broadly trimmed around the windows and between the floors with slabs of the same marble. Except for an ornate landing and doorway at the level of the water it was otherwise unadorned. The motor cut and they drifted toward the landing as though they were sliding on a sheet of black glass.

Their driver got out and steadied the boat. Celia stepped up beside him and held out her hand. Mrs. Sheridan took hold of it, ignoring the man. There would be no tip. Their luggage was brought up from the boat and she paid the fare exactly—in dollars. She always used American currency, figuring other money at the highest black market rate, because, as she said, she knew *they* did. She even carried rolls of new coins in order to make exact change, disliking to underpay as well as overpay. When she felt that she had carried out her part of the bargain—and her part was always the same—she was freer to criticize how everyone else carried out his.

During the transaction the door of the house was opened and a somber man in a striped cotton jacket and white gloves came forward and bowed. Celia gave their names but he did not reply. When the old lady had made it clear to their "gondolier" that he could take or leave what she offered him she turned and entered the house. The butler picked up their bags and waited for the girl to precede him. He returned for the small trunk and as the door closed behind him she heard the Cris-craft roar to furious life. She was afraid of meeting a victim of one of Mrs. Sheridan's bargains some day when she was alone and defenseless.

They entered a large reception room. Here the butler murmured something unintelligible, put down their bags and left through a door that was set into a mass of painted foliage. Mrs. Sheridan looked around impatiently. "Someone *might* have met us. You didn't forget to wire the time we were coming?"

"No, Mrs. Sheridan. I said four o'clock." She looked at her watch. "It's just four ten now."

"Someone should be here!"

Someone has been here, Celia thought. But of course the butler wouldn't have full status as a human. She did not particularly mind the injustice, merely the inaccuracy. To get along with Mrs. Sheridan one had to see events through her eyes, which meant distorting the most elementary facts. "But if Mr. Fox is ill," she said, "he can't be expected to greet you."

"Of course he's ill," the old lady said, as though the matter were in dispute. She paused, watching her employee's face. "And I find your tone disagreeable."

She was being ordered to apologize. Celia did not mind. When she left Mrs. Sheridan it would not be for a reason as petty as this. "I'm sorry," she said. "I expect I'm tired from the trip."

The woman's expression clearly said, "*You're* tired!" But she was satisfied. It was pleasant to hear that a young girl had less stamina than she. Celia intended it to be. She had been trained for this job for many years.

The girl turned slowly, examining the painted walls. The room was odd—not fanciful as it first appeared, but deliberately, soberly unreal. It was not simply a joke to place a false window, "through" which could be seen the canal outside the house, at exactly the point where a real window would have given the same view. And the novelty of painted mirrors and furniture wasn't worth the pains that had gone into these. Something else was meant; a kind of contempt for what was natural, and a fear of it. And then she recognized Death again. She read it in the faces of the women whose portraits had been placed in the mirrors; and she could see it in the "window," among the lifelike people sitting in the gondola. She remembered a vase of artificial flowers which her grandmother had kept on the dining room table all year long; for if they were a little stiff and colorless in summer, at least they did not wilt in winter. But Celia had always disliked them because they *weren't* flowers, ever. Even Death was not as unkind to flowers as her grandmother had been.

"Are you sure you sent the telegram?"

"What? Oh—yes, I'm quite sure."

"You might stop your wool-gathering a moment and go see what's happened. I don't much like the idea of waiting here all afternoon."

"Someone's bound to come in a moment."

"Please do as I say. I won't wait any longer."

"Yes ma'am." As she spoke the door opened and a dark young man entered. He glanced quickly at Celia, then turned to the older woman.

"Mrs. Sheridan?" His voice was light and confident.

"Yes?" Far from being pleased by his coming, the old lady was more irritable than ever. She had been kept waiting too long for her self-respect and not long enough to demand an apology.

"My name is William Fieramosca, Mr. Fox's personal secretary."

"We were afraid we'd been misdirected," Mrs. Sheridan said, coldly.

"And this is Miss Johns?"

"My companion," the woman snapped. The word was pronounced with a capital *C*.

"I'll show you to your rooms." He turned in the doorway and beckoned to the butler to take their bags.

"First I shall see Mr. Fox."

"I'm afraid not now," he said, regretfully.

Mrs. Sheridan's rice-powdered hand made a familiar gesture of dismissal. "I've come all the way from Switzerland. He wishes to see me."

The young man's voice was grave. "You've been more than kind to come. But Mr. Fox has suffered another attack this morning. Any excitement would be—dangerous."

"I'll be the judge of that! I'm an old friend."

Mr. Fieramosca seemed amused. "I know you are, Mrs. Sheridan."

She paused. "You are *not* going to take me? Your employer will be very angry when he hears of this."

"He already knows you are here. He asks if you will be kind enough to wait until this evening. I should add that he is very pleased that all of you could come."

The old lady opened her mouth to speak, then stopped. Her anger vanished. "All. . . ?"

Mr. Fieramosca glanced again at Celia. "Mr. Voltor, Mr. Sims and yourself."

"There—are others?" Her face was drawn. She seemed suddenly tired.

"I assumed you knew. He wishes to die—I think we must use the word as frankly as he does—with his closest friends around him."

Mrs. Sheridan took Celia's arm. "When did they arrive?"

"Mr. Voltor last night and Mr. Sims this morning. It was wonderful that you could all come so quickly." Again Celia caught the hidden laughter.

"I came the moment I received his letter, naturally. Unfortunately it was addressed to my bank and there was some delay."

"I'm sure Mr. Fox will understand." Mr. Fieramosca leaned forward. "*They* haven't seen him either—not yet."

Mrs. Sheridan's hand tightened on Celia's arm. "He is —*very* ill?"

The young man touched his heart. "Very." His eyes were solemn.

She straightened. "We will go to our rooms now."

He stepped back from the doorway. "That is the wisest course, Mrs. Sheridan. I promise you." His manner was faintly conspiratorial.

"And . . ."

"Yes?" He seemed to beg for her confidence.

"I wish you to come to my room in an hour. I have something to discuss with you." She moved her head slightly toward Celia and Mr. Fieramosca smiled.

"Certainly."

"You have been with Mr. Fox a long time?"

"Long enough to understand a great many things about him, Mrs. Sheridan."

"Good."

"Yes," he agreed. "I hope you will depend on me."

Celia was delighted with her room. Mr. Fieramosca had said that it was directly below the old gentleman's sickroom and had asked her not to make unnecessary noise. His manner was too solemn, as though death had no reality unless one spoke of it softly and held one's face quite expressionless. It increased her feeling that what lay on the surface in this house was more important than what was underneath. She went to the window. She had a view of the canal and the wall of Mr. Fox's garden. The plumed mimosa tree stretched toward her window, but she was disconcerted to find that it, too, looked false, even clumsily overdone. From the moment she had put foot in this city (but one didn't "put foot" in Venice—not at first) the line between truth and falsehood had grown steadily more blurred. Her own room was like a candy box and she had to remind herself that the round-bellied commode across which danced a wanton shepherdess pursued by a satyr was also fitted with drawers to hold her underclothes and blouses; and the large armoire which displayed a garden with childish ladies playing games, a greyhound beside a fountain, and two scarlet birds parading in the grass, was there principally to hold her dresses and her one practical suit. Cupids hid in a mirror on which so much colored glass was placed that it was nearly impossible to find her face. Her bed, at least, was high and solid, looking very much like a bed; but when she tried it she was astonished to see that the ceiling was covered with mirrors, cut and set in such a variety of angles that her reflection was repeated infinitely. Nor was her room conventionally shaped; it was octagonal and seemed designed to confuse all sense of direction. Nevertheless she was delighted by it. She felt pampered.

The only thing wrong was that a connecting door tied her to Mrs. Sheridan. This had once been a dressing-room, Mr. Fieramosca said. She did not resent serving the old lady, rubbing her back at night and getting up at three to give her her second pill; but when Celia was free she liked to be out of reach, if only for an hour. Here, particularly, she wanted to imagine that this was all hers. Part of the effect of this house, she had noticed, was to increase her sense of possessiveness. For the first time she began to see the person who owned it. Before, he had been merely a name, Cecil Fox, a man who was about to die. Mrs. Sheridan had never described him in any other way, and she'd had the impression when the letter arrived in Lausanne that there was very little else to know about him. But now she was beginning to feel his presence; in the garden beyond the canal, in his frescoed Steigler-Otis elevator, and his wood-paneled bathrooms with glass-enclosed showers. Finally, there was Mr. Fieramosca (Mr. Proudfly, it would be in English, if her rudimentary Italian was correct) whom surely no ordinary man would hire as a secretary. He was incongrous here, like an evening jacket at high noon. The most peculiar thing about him was that he seemed to enjoy his work, as though it were really deep sea diving or counterfeiting rather than handling correspondence and keeping accounts.

Celia checked her vanity case to see that she had enough rubbing alcohol for Mrs. Sheridan this evening. The old lady would be tired and would want extra attention. She wondered what she had wanted to see Mr. Fieramosca about. And who were the "others" whose presence had upset her so? She shook the talcum can. She would have to go into town tomorrow (did one say that about this city?) and buy some more. And sleeping pills . . . the subterfuge she had to use to protect the woman's health! Every night she had to wake Mrs. Sheridan to give her a second pill. During the first week she had worked for the old lady she decided she could not give another barbiturate with a good conscience. So she bought sugar pills and placed them in one of the old bottles. By giving the real medicine at bedtime and the false at three o'clock she kept the woman happy and at the same time prevented her from getting too much of the drug. But she knew that if she were discovered she would be fired.

Again she thought of Mr. Fox . . . about to die. "I think we must use the word as frankly as he does," Mr. Fieramosca had said. That was right. She knew something about death. No one should be too afraid of it, or life stopped having any meaning.

Her musing was interrupted by knocking on the wall to her right—the one opposite Mrs. Sheridan's room. She straightened slowly from the vanity case. Then she relaxed. It was not a human noise; it was random, senseless. She turned and noticed for the first time a small door set waist-high in the wall, so ornately decorated as to be nearly invisible in this equally ornate room. She walked to it and pulled at a grinning satyr's head. The door snapped open and she saw a taut rope waving. Occasionally it slapped against the sides of the hollow passage leading up through the wall. A simple dumbwaiter. Probably connected to Mr. Fox's . . .

Then she saw the contents of the loaded shelf as it passed on the way up. A silver bowl of ice, a bottle of Old Dan'l bourbon and, lying beside the bottle, a book. Its paper cover displayed a man with telescope arms and the head of a beetle. He was . . . Celia closed the door slowly.

He was eating a half-dressed girl.

CHAPTER FOUR

Cecil Fox stood before the fireplace in his bedroom, warming his slippered feet. A fireman-red handkerchief peeked from the pocket of his robe. His bed was disordered and the night-table beside it was prominently littered with pharmaceuticals. He drew an alligator cigar case from his pajama pocket.

"Well, bring on the Greeks," he said to his secretary, who was scenting the room with antiseptic.

"I wouldn't smoke if I were you."

The old man grinned. "Ruin my health?"

William threw some of the liquid on the fire. "The air of a sickroom isn't supposed to smell of seventy-five cent havanas."

Mr. Fox looked at the case longingly. "*You* could have been smoking."

"No I couldn't." He returned the antiseptic bottle to the night-table.

"They'd never notice," he said, petulantly.

"You'd better give the cigars to me for the time being." William held out his hand.

"Nonsense, I . . ."

"I'm sorry, the little things count most. It's a good deal harder than you think to set an illusion."

Mr. Fox handed him the cigars reluctantly. "I didn't ask for a production of Hamlet."

"You'll be lucky to get Punch and Judy."

The old man poured three fingers of golden liquid from a medicine bottle into a white hospital glass. "You take things too seriously. No sense ruining all the fun." He put the bottle back on the mantel.

William smiled. "I like to think of myself as a professional."

"Well don't bust a gut. Where's my ice bag?"

"Under your pillow. You're going to have to take something for your breath, too."

Mr. Fox carried the glass to his bed and reached beneath the pillow. "You sure this is just professional interest?"

"What else would it be?"

He unscrewed the top of the bag and fished out a chunk of ice for his drink. "I thought maybe you were beginning to join in. You've seen the three idiots. Aren't they everything I said?"

William transferred the brown bottle from the mantel to its proper place. It was appropriately marked ☠ "*veleno.*" "Your practical jokes are your own business. You hired me to put on a show. That's what I'm doing."

"To hell with that! You don't understand, boy. These people would believe I was going to die if they saw me running the four minute mile around St. Mark. They *want* to believe it."

William walked to one of the windows which gave on the square at the front of the house. Chimney swifts circled above the baroque church opposite, black wings knifing through the evening light. "It would be a mistake to assume their stupidity, sir."

Mr. Fox laughed. "Stupid is as stupid does. Isn't there a proverb like that in English?"

"Handsome."

"Eh? Oh—handsome. Sure. Well, it works with stupid, too. These people think I'm going to die and leave them a pack of money. It's so filled up their heads that they can't think of anything else. It's money they're after, Willy. M-O-N-E-Y. I picked them for that—they came for that—and now they're going to perform for that."

"But they *already* have money."

"Of course they have. That's why they want more."

The young man pulled the shutters closed, filling the room with shadows. "Have you ever considered, Mr. Fox, how easily a man may be carried away by his own cynicism?"

Cecil Fox snorted. "You have to believe too many things to be cynical. I'm telling the simple truth. From your point of view, of course, they have all the money they want. From theirs, they have almost nothing."

William turned. "And you think they're ready to jump through hoops to get it?"

"They've already jumped."

"I see. And they'll go on? It might be a little dangerous if they stopped."

The old man chewed a piece of ice noisily. He spoke at last, across cold teeth. "The secret of making a fool of a person, Willy, is to get him started. Then he prefers to go on being one rather than admit to himself what he's been."

William looked at his employer sharply. "What do you gain by it?"

"Gain? What does a man gain when he goes out and shoots defenseless birds, or chases all afternoon after a smelly little fox. Sport, boy. The poor have work to divert them. The rich depend on sport."

William began to rearrange the covers on the bed. "What's this," he said, pulling a book from the folds.

"*Il Falco degli Spazi.*"

The young man looked distastefully at the beetle-headed monster. "*The Space Falcon.* Do you have to read science fiction in the language of Dante?"

"The only reason I do is that I can't find enough of it in the language of Shakespeare," Mr. Fox said maliciously.

"Well, you can't be seen reading this. A man on the verge of death doesn't—"

"How do you know?" the old man interrupted.

William put the book in his pocket. "I don't. But it doesn't *seem* right."

"Neither does dying, I suppose." Cecil Fox shrugged off his robe. His cream silk pajamas were printed with huge purple flowers. His secretary had not been able to make him change to clinical white—and the shocking colors at least had the virtue of detracting from the patient's ruddy complexion. "O.K. Who's first?"

"Mr. Voltor. He came last night and I don't think I can hold him back any longer."

Mr. Fox chuckled and crawled into bed. "You followed my instructions?"

"Yes. The old lady spoke to me this afternoon. They've all reacted as you predicted."

"Make you any offers?"

"Nothing definite. Each one expects me to be his or her personal emissary to your bedside, and each agrees that I'll be rewarded when he inherits." William gave a last look around the room. "But since none of them has given the others credit for similar schemes, I don't think the figures they have in mind are very high—yet."

"Very well. Send in Voltor. You don't have to stay. Interrupt us in ten minutes. I'm too weak to talk longer."

"Yes sir." William went to the door.

"And for God's sake, bring back my cigars—and my book. You eat with *them* tonight. I think you've got tongue with a sweet-and-sour sauce. Second-string food. I'm having a bouillabaisse with the damned whitest wine you ever saw. Come up after dinner and we'll have another hand of poker. I'll give you an armagnac that'll break your heart."

"Not unless you need me, Mr. Fox. I'd like to go into the city."

"Secretary's night off?"

"Something like that."

"What about that girl who came with grandma Hell? Is she bearable?"

"Easily."

"Well?"

"Well, maybe."

"What do you mean, maybe? Has she got blackheads?"

William began to smile. "On her they'd be beauty marks. Come to think of it, we're going to the movies. I know just the one."

A short while later Henry Voltor was seated at Cecil Fox's bedside. He was painfully aware of the invalid's floral nightwear, but this merely confirmed his belief that the friend of his youth would not live long. As he had little experience with death (beyond that of all the intimate members of his family) he did not know how to begin. With one of his own class, or even his own nation, he might have hidden his ignorance of eternal truths behind the suggestion that they were un-British. But this man, though educated, was still an American and might expect violent commiseration. Henry winced.

"You must not, Henry. You must not," came a weak voice.

"Not what?"

"Suffer for me. I didn't ask you here for that."

Henry shifted uncomfortably. "Steady on." He looked desperately around the room. "If there's anything I can do . . ."

"No-nothing. Just now, nothing."

"Frightful shock." He looked down at his small hands. "I don't know what to say," he added, truthfully.

"Say—nothing." There was a long, dry wheeze.

"Your letter was forwarded to my club. It was . . . damned moving." Henry's face grew bright red. "Seems like yesterday, doesn't it?"

Cecil's eyes opened quickly. "What seems like yesterday?"

"Well . . ." He paused. Nothing seemed like yesterday. Even yesterday. ". . . youth, I suppose. Do you often think of . . ." He'd forgotten the blasted girl's name.

"Polly?"

"Yes. The one with the locomotives. A charming creature," he added quickly, remembering that they had both been in love with her.

The head moved feebly on the pillow. "No—not Polly. She was steel. Foundries . . ." The voice trailed off. Then it gathered strength. "You mean Helena?"

"Yes, of course. Helena. All so long ago."

Again the eyes popped open. "But like yesterday."

"Quite." He tried cheerful nostalgia. "When hearts were young and gay, eh?"

The patient smiled wanly and raised his hand to his heart.

Henry was distressed. "Sorry. I should have remembered." It occurred to him that he had never known what Cecil's disease was.

"Please, please don't apologize. I am quite prepared."

"Have you—known for long?"

"Nearly a month. The doctors can do nothing."

"You are certain?"

"Ah, my friend—death is the only certainty."

"Yes, but I mean . . ."

". . . if I am certain I shall die in a short while?"

Henry's gesture indicated both that this was what he had meant and quiet reassurance in case the answer was "yes."

"Only too soon, I'm afraid. I have been given a month, but I know this was meant as . . . encouragement."

He remembered a favorite phrase of his charwoman. "The important thing is not to give up hope."

The sick man gently closed his eyes. "The important thing," he said at last, "is to make sure."

"Yes, of course." The visitor paused, waiting for more. Finally he said, tentatively, "ah—sure of what?"

Cecil sighed. "Sometimes—I think I am the richest man in the world."

There was no response.

"I am leaving three friends in the world. Three trusted friends." The face turned on the pillow. In Henry's mind it seemed incurably ravaged. "Is there any greater wealth than that?"

"I dare say not."

"Fortunately, they are all—provided for. They do not need my physical possessions."

His face grew pale. "But surely . . ."

Cecil sighed. "I only wish one of them needed me."

As a child Henry Voltor had tried many times to step on his shadow. It was one of those games meant to accustom a boy to the world. You raised your foot and the shadow approached, but you had only to put it down again and it jumped away. If he admitted now that he was in need, the prize came within his reach. But by the same movement he betrayed the falseness of his position and the shadow escaped him forever. So he replied, "Hmmm."

"I've thought, of course, of dividing the money equally but the holdings would lose half their value if they were liquidated."

The visitor looked shocked. "Wouldn't do that, old man." His voice was charged with the sincerity of a thousand years of ruthless denial to younger sons.

Cecil brought himself up on his arms, squandering precious strength. "I *could* leave it to a charitable foundation, couldn't I?"

"Oh certainly—though one hears stories . . ."

"Stories, yes." He reached a limp hand toward the night-table.

Henry jumped up. "Here! Let me. You should have a nurse."

"No!" The soft command brought him back to his chair like a chain at his neck. "I like to do little things for myself. It's all I have." His hand closed around a glass. "What I need," he said, sipping the honey-colored medicine, "is advice."

His guest leaned forward. "Ah—I'm a solicitor, you know."

Cecil lay back on the pillow and smiled. "Thank you. I do thank you. But it's not that kind of advice I need."

Henry looked disappointed. "Yes?"

"I've almost decided to make one of you three my heir. I'm sure the others will understand my reasons—don't you believe so?"

"Undoubtedly."

"But . . ." Cecil raised his head again and drained his glass, shuddering somewhat afterwards. "I don't know which of you is—closest. Do you see?"

"Oh my, yes." Henry's manner was almost jaunty. "Only natural."

"Not that I think less of the other two," his host continued, "but they would be just a little less 'right.' Don't you agree?"

"I'm sure they'll see that."

Cecil sighed. "I'm glad you think so. I mean that you *really* think so."

"Oh, I do. Most certainly."

"I was worried that you might not understand. After all, it isn't as though you *needed* it. I mean, if I should decide that someone else . . ."

Henry frowned. The shadow teased again. He turned to look at the fire casting mocking lights into the room. "Perhaps none of us does, as you say. I haven't had the pleasure of meeting Mr.—Sims, is it?—and Mrs. Sheridan, but your man has spoken of them. Bright chap."

"Yes. He's been invaluable. You will meet my friends at dinner tonight, of course. I'd give anything in the world to be with all of you, but . . ." He closed his eyes.

Henry stood up. "I understand. I'm afraid I've tired you."

Cecil's voice was distant. "No—it makes no difference."

"By the way—I've brought you a little gift. I'll send your secretary up with it. Curious piece. It's said to have belonged to Henry VIII. One can't always believe these stories, I'm afraid, but at any rate its antiquity is attested."

The invalid raised his hand. "Good night, old friend."

Henry continued, desperately. "It's supposed to contain gold dust instead of sand. Probably untrue, but . . ." He *knew* it was true but a lifetime's habit of understatement cannot be wiped out in one afternoon.

Cecil had not opened his eyes. His guest stood over him for a moment, waiting for a crumb of gratitude. The room was silent. At last he turned to go. When he reached the door he heard a weak voice. "Ah, Henry—what is it? You must tell me what the gift is. So thoughtful!"

"An hourglass," he said, gravely, as Mr. Fieramosca tapped his ten minute warning on the other side of the door.

During the next half hour the two other friends of Cecil Fox came to see him. They were led to contemplate vast riches and politely informed of their competition. They, too, brought gifts. Mr. Sims presented his childhood friend with a lifetime, many-jeweled chronometer, set in a precious case. Mrs. Sheridan gave her former lover an enamel clock which had once counted the fleeting hours of Marie Antoinette and an unfortunate king of France.

CHAPTER FIVE

By peeping tirelessly through a knife-edged opening in his door Anson found Henry Voltor's room. It was directly down the hall from his own. The man had a certain unobtrusive dignity which he admired and despaired of emulating. He was surely English. That would have been apparent even if Mr. Fieramosca had not told him. The Sims family had occupied the United States for several hundred years and Anson regarded the English with the superstitious awe and distaste felt by the early Christians for the Jews.

When he was sure the hall was empty he slipped out and hurried toward the other door. His knock was a model for conspirators.

"Yes?" It was that naked "yes" reserved for servants and children.

Anson stepped in and shut the door behind him like a safe. "Mr. Voltor?" he said, hoarsely.

"Oh." The tone changed. "May I help you?" The question was automatic—not a real offer of help.

He bent forward to make himself shorter. "My name is Sims. Anson Sims. My room is next to yours and I felt we should know each other."

"Yes, of course." Henry's expression grew vague.

"I thought we *must* meet," Anson said, significantly.

"No doubt."

"May I sit down?"

"Please." "Don't" was implied.

Anson lunged across the room with that purposeful air with which many tall men hide a towering indecision. "You've spoken to Cecil?" he said, after he had jack-knifed into a chintz armchair.

Voltor glared at the jutting knees and nodded. "I have. What did you want to see me about?"

Sims paused. "Have you seen *her?*"

"Her?"

"Mrs. Sheridan. Didn't the young man tell you? She . . ."

Henry nodded curtly. "Yes. He told me." He disliked gossips.

Anson looked wise. "*I* have."

"Seen her?"

"Yes. This afternoon. When they arrived." He smiled knowingly. "I was looking out of the window."

Voltor chose a chair, reluctantly. "I see. Exactly what was it you wished to tell me?"

Anson glanced heavenward. " 'Better is a little with rightousness than great revenues without right,' Proverbs sixteen, eight."

"I'm sure. But you did have something else to say, didn't you?" He looked toward the door.

"She had a young girl with her," Anson said, lowering his voice.

Henry's fingers drummed on the arm of his chair. "That is most interesting, but . . ."

"You don't understand." He looked at the Englishman slyly, not knowing how far he should trust their common language. "A young and *pretty* girl. She is called a companion, I believe."

"Perhaps she is called so because she is," Voltor said, staring at the intruder's clothing.

"Yes, but for whom!" Anson said, triumphantly.

"Good heavens, *I* don't know whose companion she is. I really . . ."

"His!" Sims said, his eyes bright with zeal.

"You mean she's his mistress?" Henry accepted immorality with the calm of one who considers proper living to be a matter of restraint, not of ignorance.

"Oh my, no . . . I didn't say . . ."

"I hardly see how that's possible. A man in his condition couldn't . . ."

"I wasn't referring to anything like that," Sims said, quickly.

"Then what *were* you referring to?"

"To *her*," he said, in a spinsterish whisper.

"Whom?" Henry had grown openly annoyed.

"Mrs. Sheridan. She brought that girl here for a purpose. You mark my word!"

Voltor showed new interest. "What purpose?"

Henry smiled. "You forget that Cecil is ill. His mind may not be all . . ." He paused.

"I understand. Go on."

"Now assume for a moment that the old lady has heard that Cecil Fox is dying and that he has no relatives. I'm trying to put myself in her place, you see."

"Yes, I see."

"She also knows that he is financially very well off. It is not hard to imagine what sort of thoughts go through her mind, is it, sir?"

"Not hard. No."

Anson nodded, solemnly. "But she is afraid that Cecil has other friends closer and dearer to him than she is. Her scheme for inheriting his money will fail unless . . ."

Henry leaned forward. He looked worried. "Yes?"

". . . unless she finds some way to turn the old man's head. She must make him forget his old friends and fill him with gratitude toward herself. What could be more effective than a pretty young girl who would sit by his bedside and stroke his hand?"

Voltor nodded, slowly.

"I thought you'd see!"

"Yes, I believe I do."

"She intends to turn him against his true friends. By using the girl she will have control of the whole house in two days. Why—she can even throw us out if she wants!"

"Do you really think so?"

"Have you ever known a ruthless woman before?"

"Oh my, yes. I had an aunt."

"Then you know what they can do. *I* did the moment I saw her. She is after all of Cecil's money. If we are in her way she'll do anything to get rid of us."

Voltor clenched weak fists. "Of course it *is* a female trick—using the girl. You may be right."

"I know I am."

"But how can you be sure?"

"I feel it." Sims pointed a baleful finger at Henry. "Why else would such a girl be brought here?"

"Doesn't she look just a bit like a companion?" Henry said, hopefully.

"Not a *lady's* companion. No."

"Certainly, it's possible. In any case . . ."

"Something must be done," Anson said, looking bold.

"Look here," Henry said, after a pause. "You're a good friend of Fox?"

"We have known each other many years," Sims said, gravely.

"I don't suppose you could tell him what they're up to?"

"Of course not. He would think I was asking for myself. I thought maybe you . . ."

Voltor shook his head. "Out of the question. What rotten luck."

"We might get to the girl?"

"No," Henry said. "She'd carry tales. How could she do better with us than she's doing already?"

"Yes. I see."

"You don't suppose we could speak to Mrs. Sheridan. After all, if we all—er—trusted each other . . ."

"I'm afraid not," Anson said. "*I* saw her. She wants *every*thing."

"Very possibly."

"Besides—dividing three ways . . ."

"Yes, of course."

"I hate to see Cecil in unscrupulous hands."

Henry nodded. "I think we understand each other. *We* might work out our differences."

Sims agreed vigorously. "It's a matter of trust."

"Quite."

"A woman, on the other hand . . ."

"Very bad."

"What can we do?" Anson looked anxiously at his new friend.

Henry pursed his lips judicially. It was one of his favorite expressions and often made him wish he had "done" more with the law. "Hmmm."

"Women like that shouldn't go on living."

"Hmmm."

Anson made an ineffectual gesture of defiance. "They should be stopped!"

"Strange."

"What's strange?"

"I was thinking of an interesting case."

Anson looked annoyed. "I came here because I thought you might have some suggestion. I . . ."

"Two nephews were living with a rich aunt and one day she fell down the service stairs and was killed."

"Killed?" Anson replied, in a subdued voice.

"Unfortunately, suspicion fell on one of the nephews. The police were about to bring him in for questioning when the other nephew covered him with an alibi. In time the police gave up, accused the first footman, and hung the poor chap, I believe." Henry looked toward the window. "Interesting."

Anson frowned. "Why weren't they both accused?"

"It is always difficult to charge two respectable men with the same crime. The presumption of innocence is twice as strong." Voltor passed an aristocratic hand through his thinning hair. "Besides, there is no reason to believe they *weren't* innocent."

Anson nodded. "But suppose they weren't. If it were planned, I mean . . ."

"Yes?"

"I say, *if* it were planned; which of the nephews would—see that the old lady fell?"

Henry smiled, coldly. "I think Americans tend to be too rigid in such matters. Your courts are choked with cases which demonstrate the wrong plan brilliantly executed at the wrong moment. In England we are more flexible."

"But surely . . ."

"Tradition of craftsmanship, probably. *If* the nephews were guilty, as you say, I'm sure they didn't decide how she was going to die beforehand; no more than they would agree which of them would kill her. On the contrary, they would leave as much to chance as possible. You must remember that the police are very adept at detecting man-made plans. Chance is a mystery to everyone."

Anson was gnawing a hangnail. "Of course," he said, "they *were* innocent."

Henry stared at his visitor. "That seems quite clear," he said with a smile which Mrs. Sheridan would not have enjoyed seeing.

CHAPTER SIX

They were to dress for dinner. For Celia this was always a double ordeal, for she had to think of Mrs. Sheridan as well as herself. The old lady wore evening clothes as she would a uniform. The slack, bare arms proclaimed victories in a hundred good hotels and odorous watering places. The jeweled choker on her wrinkled neck was a badge of authority. Her clothing was always chosen to display social power. This was especially true of the gowns she wore after dark, though she and her companion might do nothing more daring than read old copies of *Town and Country* in the lounge. For herself, Celia was condemned to wear either her old chiffon or her cocktail dress with the very long skirt. Even if she'd had the money to buy something better she would not have dared. Mrs. Sheridan was not paying her to "show off," a code phrase she used when she spoke of those who drew attention from herself.

But long ago Celia had learned to overcome disagreeable moments in her life by a method which was as practical as it was lonely. She merely turned to herself, as to an old friend, and entered a world which never hesitated to welcome her. Not that she dreamed impossibilities. She credited herself with little imagination and had no taste for cheap posturing. This private world contained nothing fantastic or silly. She simply found, whenever she was quiet for a moment, that ordinary events grew charged with extra meaning. A woman walking across a lawn was obviously about to cry, a man signing a restaurant check was wondering if he had enough money to pay his bill, a child alone at a table was steering a ship, an old woman coveted a plate of ice cream, a captive blackbird imitated the whistle of a busboy. Others might ignore the commonplace moments of a day or an evening, but for her they were everything. A person who was not "a member of life," as she called it, valued the smallest things most. That was why she had known immediately that the strange supplies she had seen going up on the dumb-waiter were for Mr. Fox. She understood how a man could drink whisky and read sensational stories on his deathbed. Through them he might still taste the life he was about to leave.

At seven she was dressed. She combed two drops of expensive and somewhat disappointing French perfume into her chestnut hair and went in to Mrs. Sheridan. The maid had done a good job with the pressing—the first hurdle. She massaged the back of the old lady's neck to bring her "peace of skin," as an enthusiastic Swiss beauty counsellor had called it. She stood patiently through the creaming and wiping ("Don't *hover*. I have no intention of hurrying on your account. I suppose you find it intolerable to help me just a little?"), and later she picked imaginary threads from a brocade bag. She searched her own room for extra pads to ease the pinch of shoes a size too small. She snapped snaps. She flattered. At eight they were ready.

Celia did not despise Mrs. Sheridan. She didn't even dislike her, beyond a moment or two—as when she was accused of finding intolerable the very thing she was obviously tolerating. She could recognize the twisted child underneath. There was nothing really threatening to her in this pointless egotism, nor in the old lady's senile rage for power. She was growing old and the threat of death sickened her. It was one of those diseases which must come very early if it is to come lightly—like measles. For it *could* come early—Celia had met Death herself when she was very young, nursing her grandmother. Now she was immune, or as much as it was ever possible to be. But Mrs. Sheridan was not. She was frightened and she hit back as though in a nightmare. The fact that she could hit only at those people who depended on her money was nearly pathetic—but not quite. The woman was too old to survive this illness—and she would never stop trying to infect everyone else.

As they were going down the hall to the elevator, Mrs. Sheridan took her arm for support. "Do you like this house, dear?"

"Dear" was most often used spitefully (why, in every language, did it also refer to a price?) but this time Celia caught a note of tenderness. Momentarily the old lady was pleased—by something . . .

"It's very lovely." She noticed that the floor tiles were printed with black boats, each bearing colored sails. ". . . and very strange," she added.

"One really ought to settle in Venice—it's so *central.*" The harsh old voice was bemused.

"Should I go back for your wrap?" Celia had detected the draft that would touch Mrs. Sheridan's shoulders just as they reached the table.

She ignored the question. "Of course it *is* in Italy."

"Of course."

The old lady looked at her sharply. "Why will you insist on painting your face like a salesgirl?"

Celia lowered her eyes, a gesture of humility which, at least, required no words.

"They've come a long way for nothing." Mrs. Sheridan chuckled and dropped her employee's arm. "If he thinks I won't speak he's got another think coming."

Celia avoided asking who. She wasn't supposed to ask questions at times like this, or even to understand too clearly—just listen.

"If he tries anything I'll bring it to court."

The elevator rose to meet them. The doors pressed back and Mr. Fieramosca stepped out. He *was* in a dinner jacket this time. He wore it just as Celia knew he would—like a magician or a band leader. She didn't consider this a valuable talent. It was merely curious . . .

"They won't have a leg to stand on."

She tried to picture a number of people standing on even one.

"What's that, Mrs. Sheridan?" The young man adjusted his smile like a cummerbund. His eyes glittered with intelligence, which was surprising. Handsome men often lacked it.

"I can't imagine that it would interest you," Mrs. Sheridan snapped. She seemed to regret the respect which she had allowed him this afternoon.

"Perhaps not. I was just coming to get you. I thought you would like a drink before . . ."

"Are you to eat with the guests, Mr. Firemouse?"

"Fieramosca," he said, quietly. "As none of you speaks Italian, that will be best, I believe. In any case . . ." He stopped as his eyes caught Celia's. She saw the anger vanish. He held the doors of the elevator open. "May I show you the way, Mrs. Sheridan . . . Miss Johns?"

The old lady brushed past. "Probably freezing in winter," she muttered. She examined the painted interior of the elevator. "Still, something may be done with it."

Celia stepped in and as Mr. Fieramosca closed the door his sleeve brushed her arm. It was deliberate, she knew—and she wondered if he had also judged the faint chill his presence caused at the back of her neck.

She found Mr. Sims and Mr. Voltor disappointing. After Mrs. Sheridan's reaction this afternoon she had expected them to be more . . . threatening. She didn't know why she should have felt immediately that they were a threat, but even now—in spite of the old lady's renewed confidence—she sensed their antagonism. Mr. Sims was tall and dry, and when he moved he seemed to rustle like a long piece of foolscap. Mr. Voltor had a large head which balanced painfully on a skinny neck. His hairline receded in two lakes of pink flesh, divided by a sandy promontory of wavy hair. His body was unimportant, neither wide nor narrow, nor any unusual height. Celia imagined it would feel like a poor cut of meat which had been cooked tender (though she was extremely sorry to imagine any such thing). There were certain men, she thought, who were satisfied simply to be males—not even impressive males; a name, a suit, a set of secondary sex characteristics were enough. Having these, they coasted; they adopted unchanging habits and rode out their lives. These two men were like that, and that was exactly what was strange about their presence. Why were they here? Certainly not because they wished to be at the bedside of a dying friend. That was unbelievable—as unbelievable as Mrs. Sheridan saying that she was here for the same purpose.

They were in Mr. Fox's library. The book bindings glistened in the light of the chandelier. A fire cut the chill coming up from the canal. Mr. Fieramosca went to a small black boy made entirely of glass and placed a finger in his left eye. Celia winced.

"I thought you'd all prefer the library to the living room," William said. "Of course, if you'd rather . . ."

Mr. Sims cleared his throat, as though it were choked with autumn leaves. "Ah—are you ordering beverages?"

Outside, Celia heard the warning cry of a gondolier coming to a bend.

"Yes sir. Do you wish anything in particular?"

"I shall have an Alexander," Mrs. Sheridan said.

Mr. Fieramosca kept his eyes on Mr. Sims.

"Plain hot water with a little tangerine juice, if you have it." Anson addressed a white smile to the lady. She had taken the most comfortable chair.

Celia stood by the window. She heard an oar splash in the darkness.

"And you, sir?"

Henry Voltor was examining the books, clearly as disinterested in literature as in the present company. "Sherry."

The door swung slowly open and the butler entered. William spoke to him for some moments in Italian and Celia heard the word "*crema*" repeated several times with mounting impatience. At last the butler nodded, in a manner which suggested a shrug, and left. She had decided she did not like Mr. Fieramosca's voice. It was artificial. He pronounced his words too clearly, his politeness was too heavily underlined.

He turned back to the others. "I know Mr. Fox will

be disappointed if you don't take advantage of his hospitality. If there is anything that you—desire, I'll do my best to see that you have it."

At the word "desire" Celia noticed a faint movement of the skin at his temples, as though he were a breath away from outright laughter.

Mr. Sims looked sour. "I can speak for no one but myself, but I shall be content with Cecil's recovery."

Both Mrs. Sheridan and Henry Voltor turned to him impatiently.

"If God wills . . ." Anson added.

William quickly bowed his head. "Perhaps—who knows?"

Henry left his solitary inspection of book leathers and joined the others. "Ah . . ." He tried hearty good cheer. "Looking up this evening, is he?"

"I don't know. It's too early to tell." Celia noticed how exactly he hit the note of restrained optimism.

Mrs. Sheridan scowled. "Speak up! How is he?"

William sighed. "I think—he's better. Your visits did him a great deal of good."

Anson examined one of the ivory chess pieces. His face had grown somber. " 'For the Lord hath given, and the Lord hath taken away.' Job one, twenty-one."

William smiled. "At any rate, He hasn't taken away—yet."

"Nor given!" Mrs. Sheridan said, staring angrily at Anson.

"What do you mean by that, madam?"

Mr. Voltor drifted toward the tapestry with his hands clasped behind his back as though he were at a museum.

"Exactly what you think I mean. You've come a long way for nothing, sir!"

William interrupted. "I imagine the trip has been tiring for everyone. At least Mr. Voltor has had a night's sleep. I'm astonished that you look so fresh, Mrs. Sheridan. Some people seem to thrive on inconvenience."

Celia was nearly envious. Mr. Fieramosca had managed to praise her employer's appearance—and consequently, health—without minimizing her hardships.

"I have never felt well in the spring," the old woman said, pleased. "I need my sleep. I can't get a good sleep in the spring."

Anson sat stiffly, coddling his indignation.

"Yes—some have more difficulty than others. Especially during this season." William's gesture said, "Yet look how you've come through it!"

He was good, Celia thought. Not extravagantly so. He didn't resort to open flattery. He played on her fear of death. Nothing could be more effective.

"Has spring come to England yet, Mr. Voltor?"

Not a band-leader, perhaps. A master of ceremonies.

Henry turned slowly. "I really couldn't say. I only notice weather in foreign countries."

"I think that's profoundly true—do you agree, Mr. Sims?"

A mournful chorus of bells echoed from surrounding church towers.

"I don't care for idle speculation," Anson replied.

"Well, of course, I understand. Have you ever visited Venice before, sir?"

"No."

Mr. Fieramosca proceeded tirelessly, without very much success, Celia felt. But at least in fighting off his questions the group began to draw together. They could no longer ignore each other. It struck Celia that the young man *knew* why these old people were here; she seemed to know also, without putting it into words.

"Mr. Fox has always been very generous with this city, I understand. Reconstruction. A lot of the foundations are giving way." William turned to the door. "In recent years he's been comparatively poor. Of course he has no heirs . . ."

The butler re-entered, bearing a silver tray with an assortment of bottles and pitchers. Mrs. Sheridan leaned forward as though a heavy wind were pressing at her back. "What did you say?"

But the young man was speaking in Italian. Celia heard the word "*crema*" again. He seemed angry.

Henry Voltor's naked forehead was waxen. "Ah—I wonder if you would . . ."

William interrupted. "I'm sorry, Mrs. Sheridan, your Alexander will have to be made with whipped cream. The butler assumed you were having a dessert and there is no more cream in the house."

Anson coughed. "Will you please explain? You say Mr. Fox was very—generous?"

William nodded to the butler, who put the tray on the table. "Oh yes, he's always been. Some people have criticized him for it. He throws money away."

Mrs. Sheridan's voice trumpeted. "You *said* he . . ."

"I'm sorry about the cream, Mrs. Sheridan. In any case, I hardly think you will notice the difference."

Henry stepped forward. "I'm afraid I'll have to ask for an explanation. You implied that—Cecil is destitute. I speak, of course, as . . ."

"An old friend?"

"Naturally."

"Perhaps you misunderstood, sir. I hope this sherry

will be all right. Mr. Fox seldom drank it. He said it was for dead-beats and old ladies. He was frequently facetious, as you know."

The old lady half rose from her chair. "I insist. . . !"

William smiled as he handed the sherry to Mr. Voltor. "I believe I said that Mr. Fox was comparatively poor."

Anson rubbed his hands nervously. "Yes—those were your words."

"As you probably know, Mr. Fox once controlled an immense fortune." He poured hot water into a glass. "I'm afraid you must tell me how much fruit juice you usually take, Mr. Sims." He tinted the water with tangerine juice and looked doubtfully at the tall man.

Henry's hand closed tightly on his glass. "Once?"

"Of course I suppose his wealth now would seem vast to many people." William wrapped a napkin around the hot drink and handed it to Anson as though it were a mild poison.

The tension slackened. Celia noticed a dark red blotch spreading on Mrs. Sheridan's neck. "To *what* people?"

"It's difficult to say. Wealth is hard to define, don't you agree? Of course, Mr. Fox is still extremely well off."

"Well off?" Henry's voice was weak.

"The phrase is confusing, I admit. I mean—rich."

Anson closed his eyes. There was a long silence. At last he murmured, " 'A good name is rather to be chosen than great riches,' Proverbs XXII, 1." Steam rose from his pale orange glass.

As they sat down to dinner Mrs. Sheridan asked Celia to run upstairs for her wrap. William offered to send one of the maids but the old lady refused, on Celia's behalf. The girl didn't mind. She was tired of hearing people use words to hide meanings rather than reveal them. She understood, now, that these three were after Mr. Fox's money. She was not shocked. It wasn't very nice, but people had been hovering around deathbeds for thousands of years for the same purpose, and she had no reason to suppose they would give up the practice during her lifetime. Except that the old gentleman upstairs was counting on them. It made no difference if they merely pretended affection for him. That way, at least, they would *earn* the money. But she doubted if they would do it very well. They were not used to earning anything—least of all money. Money. Celia stopped and touched a long crystal hanging like an earring from a wall lamp. She wondered what it would be like to be very rich. . . .

Long ago there was a dance floor, lit by the morning sun. Couples waited awkwardly while one of the older girls wound a portable phonograph. The machine was covered with that neat, striped material which gives anything with a handle the right to be called "airplane luggage." The girls of the sophomore class at Lincoln High, in a moment of extraordinary generosity (slightly marred by condescension), had invited the girls of the graduating class of Irving Junior for a morning's fun at Capitol Park. They had bumped each other in little red cars. They had drunk root beer and screamed all the way round the ferris wheel. And they had danced at eleven o'clock in the morning with sunlight streaming through the pavilion. There were boys—chosen by the chaperones—and there was music. Sweet, slick, sentimental music.

There had been talk of dates—and the older girls spoke mysteriously of sororities and mixed parties which lasted until two A.M. They had seemed grown women, Celia remembered. They wore lipstick without being embarrassed. Their heels were very thin and high. The music flowed, suggesting bouquets of flowers, long dresses, and knowing laughter. There was also an older boy in white slacks (it was June, the month of graduations and weddings) who looked something like Robert Taylor. Dark hair and serious eyes, but very small and badly formed ears. She hadn't danced with him. It was inconceivable that anyone but a woman would dare to. In fact, she had danced only once, with Junior Mutz of her class. The rest of the time she stood by the phonograph and watched.

She hadn't wanted to come. She'd told her grandmother that she hardly knew anyone. But the old lady had insisted, perhaps feeling guilty for keeping her away from other parties. Her dress was not right. Her black shoes were irreparably scuffed. But she was glad she was there, if only to see the life that lay before her . . . A continuous swirling under a pink ceiling, a soft crying of clarinets. She thought of streamlined cars, of monogrammed silver cigarette lighters (of course she would be smoking). "$^{C}{}_{J}$" or a simple "C.J."? She gripped her hands in the folds of her dress while the metallic music unwound. She dreamed. Loneliness was banished—for the first time in her life and the last . . .

The music died, the Irving girls were escorted home by their chaperones and, slowly, the flurry of graduation subsided. When, three months later, she began her classes at Lincoln, grandma had grown much worse and the few friendships she depended on dissolved like summer ant hills under fall rains. Later, she was not sorry. The whimpering clarinets, the teardrop cars, the silver lighters (she smoked now and used matches) were not for her. She would not have been happy in that cotton-candy world, even if it had been offered to her. But in the back of her mind the impossible music of that June morning still sounded and the image of the dark young man flickered. She did not want *that*, but she would like, at least, to have the chance to refuse it. Celia remembered the old man upstairs. If she were rich—terribly rich—she might become, for a month or even a year, the person she had dreamed of being long ago. She suddenly thought of Mr. Fieramosca with his too handsome face and his sharp, inquiring eyes. She had stopped in the hallway outside Mrs. Sheridan's room. Her ears stung with shame. How could she condemn those people downstairs? What would *she* do if she had a chance to inherit a great deal of money?

She brought the wrap into the dining room and placed it around Mrs. Sheridan's shoulders. The bare back was wrinkled like the surface of a cup of hot milk.

"My dear woman," Anson said. "I have traveled here at great inconvenience and . . . And I will not allow you to suggest . . ."

The old lady raised her eyebrows. ". . . that you're a hyprocrite?"

Celia saw Mr. Fieramosca motion to the footman. He began to take away the thick soup plates, leaving her own. The young man was making no attempt to stop the argument. Instead, he listened carefully to Mrs. Sheridan. He appeared worried.

"And you're no better, Mr. Voltor. I've met your type before."

"Type? Good heavens, is there?" His face was calm, but Celia saw his hands tremble as he raised the napkin lightly to his lips.

"You think you're better than everyone, but you're not. You connive and scheme like . . ." She searched her private rogue's gallery of schemers. "Like a Frenchman!" she said, triumphantly.

Mr. Voltor clamped his teeth and guided a row of crumbs across the table cloth with his knife. The footman reached past him with spotless gloves and with the edge of a folded napkin brushed the particles into a silver dish.

"You came here for nothing, both of you! *I* know."

William glanced at her sharply.

Mr. Sims' eyelids were half-lowered. "I'm sure you do, madam."

Celia's soup was served and she began to eat it quickly, not only to catch up, but to keep from looking at Mr. Fieramosca.

Mrs. Sheridan's voice rose. "You don't believe me? I'll take the wind out of your sails! It's lucky I came in time."

William spoke. "Please go on, Mrs. Sheridan."

"All right. I would have preferred to keep certain things to myself—but I won't see these two scavengers pull the wool over honest people's eyes any longer!"

Celia caught a faint glint in Mr. Fieramosca's eye. She wondered if he was thinking of wool-pulling scavengers.

"Yes?" The young man gestured to the footman to take Celia's plate. Her employer hadn't noticed that the meal was being held up while she finished the first course.

Mr. Voltor leaned forward. "If you wish, you *may* keep them to yourself."

Anson took a pill from a ragged matchbox. "Have you any bottled water?" he said to William.

Mr. Fieramosca turned quickly and ordered *acqua*

minerale. Then he looked again at Mrs. Sheridan. "Please, you wished to explain something?"

"I certainly do. If Cecil won't, I will—for his own good. I'm an old woman now . . ." She looked quickly to Celia for some gesture of denial. ". . . and my reputation is what I've made it. Cecil Fox is my husband!"

The footman tipped the green bottle above Anson's glass. Celia saw Mr. Fieramosca start, as though he had received a slight blow in the face. Slowly, he smiled. "I think I understand, Mrs. Sheridan. There are certain—indiscretions the world tolerates. Your relationship to Mr. Fox was no casual one, obviously. But that hardly makes you his wife."

The old woman's color had grown very high. "Oh, but it does! I have been told very definitely that it does, if I care to claim it. I'd hoped it wouldn't be necessary, but before I see these *carrion* . . ." She glared across the table. Anson placed a pill on his tongue and washed it down, hastily. Carrion, Celia thought, abstractly, is not the eater but the eaten. ". . . lay their hands on . . ."

Mr. Voltor spoke with difficulty. "Quite, madam. You've made your views clear. What Mr. Fera-Moscow wishes to know is whether you and Cecil Fox are man and wife in the sight of God, or of some more temporal agency."

"And more accessible to courts," William said, choosing a white wine. "My name is Fieramosca," he said to Henry, with patient emphasis.

Anson closed his matchbox and snapped a rubber band around it. "How do you claim to be his wife when you call yourself by another name?"

Celia felt almost proud of her employer. She had not suspected her of such a dubious past. "When I knew him," the woman said, "his name was Sheridan. I was known as his wife. By *everyone*. Do you understand?"

Anson smirked. "That's all very well—but were you?"

"There was no ceremony . . ." She touched her jeweled choker for assurance. ". . . but that was quite unnecessary."

"No doubt," Henry said, stiffly.

Mr. Fieramosca was frowning. "You lived together in the United States?"

"Yes."

"And you have witnesses? Living witnesses?"

Mrs. Sheridan nodded. "I'm not *that* old, young man. What is more, there is enough documentary evidence to prove it any time I please." She smiled bitterly. "There is nothing more final than a small town society column, I assure you."

William examined his fork. "You are referring to common-law marriage, I gather."

"But that's ridiculous! The courts would throw it out. God knows how many years it's been since she . . ." Anson looked at the old woman with distaste.

The young man shook his head. "Perhaps not, Mr. Sims. Over twenty states still recognize common-law marriage, and a marriage once established endures until the law—or death—dissolves it. If Mrs. Sheridan can prove 'open and notorious cohabitation,'—I believe that's the phrase—in a state which admits common-law marriage, she is undoubtedly his wife."

"Exactly." Mrs. Sheridan said, "I've been told that it will stand as a valid marriage if I wish to make a claim. I'd rather not resort to it, but I will if necessary. Poor Cecil may not be in his right mind, and I will not allow these jackals to hoodwink him!"

Henry drummed on the table. "Of course the final decision rests with Mr. Fox."

"That is just where it does *not* rest, sir! I will contest every will my husband makes which does not make me sole beneficiary. I may not win but I can hold up settlement for years."

"Haven't you all forgotten one thing?" Mr. Fieramosca's eyes were shining with laughter.

They looked at the young man apprehensively.

"Mr. Fox isn't dead yet."

And once again Celia felt the presence of an old friend in the house. The soft, almost shy, presence of Death. It had entered the room, approached the table and touched them all. Then it lingered with her, as old friends will.

CHAPTER SEVEN

Cecil Fox was propped up in his bed, waiting for company. The bouillabaisse was not sitting well and even the *blanc du blanc* moiled a bit, so he was not patient. The remains of his meal had been taken away and the door left unlocked. If he could predict their reactions to meeting each other tonight—and so far he was doing pretty well—one, at least, would weaken enough to come to him. Because his stomach had disappointed him it was all the more important that his mind should not. He deserved *some* pleasure out of the evening. The room was dim. Necessary, of course, but annoying. He remembered what William had said about two kinds of darkness. Cecil kicked at his blanket and belched. There was a gentle knock.

He lay his head against the pillow and turned his eyes to the doorway. The knock was repeated but he did not answer. Long ago, when he was young, a professional poker player had told him, "It's never too soon to start winning. You don't have to play at all; but if you do, start before the sucker gets in the door. Only a damn fool waits until he sees his cards." So the evening was going to be a success, after all. The thought even improved his digestion. He said nothing.

Again a knock. Soft at first and then more resolute—or desperate. Cecil grinned. It wasn't difficult to guess who it was. He imagined the man trembling behind the door, promising himself to go away after one more knock. Oh lovely! He was sorry he hadn't begun playing this years ago. Monkey on a string. With a real monkey and a gold string. Knock knock knock, tap tap. Let him go on till October. There was a pause. Cecil was afraid he had ducked, but he kept quiet. In an hour, or a day, he'd be back sweating more than ever. True pleasures were always worth waiting for. That was how you knew them. The door handle moved downward.

Anson Sims peered in. He looked like a trusted bank clerk who has just broken into the vault. In school he had been known as "The Raven" because of a sepulchral and somehow indignant reading he had given Poe's poem. Cecil pretended not to recognize him. He had always wondered how the righteous looked while committing crimes. Did the minister seem unworthy of his pulpit as he made a pass at the sexton's wife? Did the philanthropist appear less of a public benefactor as he stole the orphan's candy? Apparently not. The personality was stronger than its actions. Sims seemed a model of probity, especially in money matters. He probably even believed he was. Cecil wondered if he saved string.

Anson cleared his throat. The dying man stared at him unblinkingly. Again. A sound for a library or a church—or a tomb. Dry, like the man.

"Are you—awake?"

The eyes regarded the visitor incuriously.

"I don't wish to intrude, but . . ."

A languid hand raised from the sheet. A new watch was strapped to the wrist. "Come near—Anson. I was expecting you."

"Expecting? But you didn't . . ."

"I mean I was counting on you." The voice faded.

Anson stepped forward, breathing in confidence. "I hope you always will."

"Always is not such a long time in my case." The hand fell back to the bed. After a long pause Cecil continued, as a virtuoso with an instrument which pleases him. "You are good, *good* to keep me company. The evenings are long." He looked away, wondering if that wasn't a trifle florid.

Anson sat stiffly on a small chair at the edge of the bed. He had cadaverous stingy hands, adapted to folding bits of paper neatly and picking up pins. It would be a real triumph to lighten his pocket.

"I felt I had to come. There is something you must know."

Cecil shook his head. "Please. There is so little time left. I want to know nothing but my friends."

"But that is what I must tell you. They are not what you think." The thin lips were set in indignation.

Cecil reached for the glass on his night table and swallowed the contents. "What I think?"

An ornate clock on the mantel struck. As Pierrot spun eleven times an enamel-faced courtier kissed Pierrette, and placed a tiny hand on her half-bared breast each time her lover's back was turned.

Cecil listened wearily as Anson unburdened his suspicious heart. Henry Voltor and Mrs. Sheridan were after money. They cared less than nothing for *him*. They were hypocrites—whited sepulchres "full of dead men's bones, and of all uncleanness." Of course, Anson regretted having to be the one to carry the unpleasant news (as the buckshot said to the backside) but he could not do less and call himself a true friend.

"You can't be serious."
"I've never been more serious in my life."
I'll bet you haven't, skinny. The fruit's hanging right over your jaws. Between slavers you tell tales on the other hyenas. And by Jehovah's Foot, I bet you don't even embarrass yourself!
"The woman claims . . ."
Cecil held up his hand. "Enough!" He managed a tremor. "I don't want to hear any more."
"But I'm telling the truth. The woman says that you and . . ."
"I won't listen. As long as they're under my roof and I'm alive no one shall speak against them. Not even you." He thought the last was a nice touch. It gave hope, but not too much.
"But I only . . ."
And the pious old fraud began to eat his own words. One by one, like persimmons. Might have been mistaken . . . it seemed so to me, but . . . as Paul said to the Romans . . .
Then he began to work around again. Couldn't be too careful . . . who, after all, was "unspotted from the world". . . he had felt it his duty to. . . . He weaved and tossed, bucked and quoted. Cecil was impressed. The man had more jisum than he'd counted on. And all for nothing. So he could put the money in the bank and let it rot. He was a saver, no mistake. He had the soul of a ragpicker.
Cecil poured another shot of armagnac from his medicine bottle.
"I think none of us form such lasting impressions as during youth. You set me an example which has guided me through . . ."

You're lucky you remembered my name, you mouldy old geek.

". . . for years I have considered myself in your spiritual debt. I *had* to come tonight. Maybe I was overscrupulous, but I couldn't act otherwise."

Oofah! *Spiritual* debt. "On examining your holy bank account we find that you have been overdrawn since March twelfth and are in our spiritual debt two hundred thousand kisses and a custom built Rolls Royce cloud."

"In many ways you and I are much alike."

Cecil nodded. "Yes—I've sensed it. That's why I don't hesitate to ask a small favor."

Anson leaned forward, eagerly. "Of course! I'd be delighted. Surely you know that."

The invalid smiled weakly. "I've just said that I did."

"Anything. Anything at all!"

"You may lend me ten thousand." Cecil sighed deeply, as though in pain.

The clock on the mantel struck the quarter hour. The courtier reached for the treasures of Pierrette's bosom.

". . . ah—lire?" The voice was shrunken, the last cry of a deflated balloon.

"Dollars. Better make it fifteen."

"Fifteen? Thousand?"

"I think that'll be enough."

"But surely you have—I mean the figure is a bit—high."

A note of suspicion entered Cecil's voice. "You *have* it, I hope."

"Have it? Why—yes. That is, in my bank. In New York. Naturally it would be impossible to . . ."

"Good. You can cash a check here tomorrow."

"But, if you could tell me the—purpose." Anson's

fingers twisted together and grew white. "I know you have perfectly good reasons, of course," he added, quickly. "But the sum is rather l-large."

Cecil had risen to a sitting posture. His eyes were cold. "If you'd rather not we needn't discuss it further."

"Oh—I would. I would! But . . ."

He began to dodge and wheel again. He hadn't devoted his life to savings for nothing. In the end he would give in, Cecil saw. But complete surrender was out of the question. He would have been just as stubborn with fifty cents. He demanded a reason. Not outright—he was too afraid of losing the borrower's blessing, *if* it was worth anything. But he would find out, first, why a millionaire wanted fifteen thousand dollars.

"I've had to let my affairs go since my illness." Cecil began to have trouble with his breath. "If I liquidate now I take a fifty percent loss. In the meantime my cash balance has . . ."

Anson brightened, but a shadow remained. "Couldn't *something* be liquidated now? Surely . . ."

"Of course," Cecil said, letting his hand fall to the sheet. "A few thousand are unimportant now." He attempted a smile. "And they mean nothing to the person who will inherit the rest."

Anson drew himself up bravely. "I will see that you have the money tomorrow morning."

For a moment Cecil's eyes seemed to mist with tears. Then he lay back and breathed deeply. "Thank you, my friend."

"I must thank *you* for allowing me to repay my debt."

The voice came from far away. "Your spiritual debt?"

"Exactly. It is a great privilege."

"Thank you. We all owe each other so much." Cecil

shut his eyes and a moment later Anson tiptoed from the room.

When the door closed, Cecil got up, fished a cigar from a covered chamber pot within the night-table and pried open the lid of a small wooden packing box. From its bed of excelsior he took King Henry's hourglass. He set it on the floor beside his bed, punched a lever of his chronometer, and sat back to time an hour's worth of gold, dropping delicately into the empty section of the glass. It occurred to him that this would be an excellent way to go to sleep.

When Anson arrived in his room he took his Bible from the shoe box which held his shaving equipment and turned to the sixth chapter of Revelation. He ran his finger quickly to the eighth verse. "And I looked, and behold a pale horse; and his name that sat on him was Death." Comforted, he closed the book and went to sleep.

CHAPTER EIGHT

The note had been delivered to her room while she was preparing to help Mrs. Sheridan to bed. The maid grinned at her as Celia took the envelope. The message was pleasingly direct. It asked her to come to the library if she were free within the next hour. "I know where a cowboy movie is playing. Or, if you can't stand excitement, I'll buy you a dish of ice cream." It was signed "Bill Fieramosca." Either the boy-next-door parody was meant to amuse her or to reassure. It did both. Celia decided to go, though she was slightly annoyed at reacting to his invitation precisely as he had intended.

She took rubbing alcohol, talcum, and the bottle of sugar pills from her dressing case. She had one real sleeping pill left in her purse, wrapped in a piece of kleenex. She could palm that and give it to the old lady first. Then she was supposed to place the bottle, together with a clean handkerchief, a flacon of baby's nose drops and a small container of lavender salts in Mrs. Sheridan's bag, put the bag on a chair beside the bed and make sure that her water glass was covered. This routine must never be varied. The woman was already fretting. She pulled at her blankets and plumped her pillows in an angry frenzy. "I must get my sleep. I must!" Celia handed her the first pill and held the glass for her. Then she arranged the other articles in the bag. The important thing was to assure her that she could have everything she wanted, that they were just within reach; but also she had to be assured that she would never *have* to reach for them. Someone would come to give them to her the moment she called.

Celia began to rub the loose back, waiting for it to grow red under the alcohol. "I must get my sleep!" the woman moaned. She said "my sleep" as though it were, "my dress" or "my ring." It *belonged* to her. Every night a certain amount. And if she "lost" it she was frantic. She had forgotten that sleep was not a thing, it was a country. You couldn't *get* it, you had to *go* there. And it was never lost. Sometimes you missed a train, but there was always another coming after. In the meantime, neither the green hills nor the nightmare forests ever changed. They stayed where they were and you went to them. And sooner or later you would go and not come back. Celia knew that this was why the old woman preferred to think of sleep as something she owned. She wanted to control it because she was afraid that it would soon control her.

She continued the massage for nearly an hour. Mrs. Sheridan seemed to know she was planning to go out. But at last the woman's breath grew deeper and she began to groan, which was her way of snoring. Celia pulled up the covers, shut off the lights and tiptoed from the room. She wasn't afraid of waking her—the pill had taken effect—but she felt guilty about leaving. *She* was young. The nights weren't a terror to her. . . . She left the door open and her own bed lamp on. Mrs. Sheridan slept best under the threat of light.

Going down in the elevator she felt uneasy, as though she were running out on her job. Celia knew that if she had asked permission to leave, the old lady would have refused. What was worse, if at that moment she had quit her job and said she was going anyway the woman would have begged her to stay. As she stepped into the first floor hall and drew the sliding doors shut, the darkness folded around her. She was grateful for it. But as she started down the hall a light came on and the door of the library swung open.

Mr. Fieramosca stepped out. "I thought maybe you didn't like cowboy pictures *or* ice cream."

She didn't answer his smile. "It would serve you right if I did."

"I don't understand. Why?"

She began to blush. "I don't know—I suppose I was thinking you wouldn't *really* like to spend the evening with a girl clipped off a box of breakfast cereal."

He frowned. "What's that got to do with it? You'd better like Westerns, anyway. *I'm* in this one. I play the heavy."

"Heavy? Oh." She stepped into the library. Of course. That explained so much. A movie villain would be more attractive in the flesh than the hero. Still . . .

"*Alza le mani,* Jack!" He pushed the door shut and clapped his hand to his thigh. His face was twisted in a conventional, though surprisingly convincing, sneer.

Celia laughed. "Does that mean hands up?" He really *did* look like a killer. She was glad she had come.

"I never knew there was so much land in Venice!" They were walking through a square which connected a number of little streets like a knot in a net. The square was lined with shops, most of them closed with steel shutters. But ahead she saw a sign: BAR–GELATERIA. There were tables in front.

"Disappointed?"

"No. Only whenever I decide anything, I find it isn't true."

"What else, for instance? Would you like your ice cream now?" He led her to the tables. At one of them a mother was administering black coffee to a child on her lap.

Celia accepted an aluminum chair. "Well—I thought you were much more . . ."

"Unpleasant?"

"No—that is, perhaps. But there's always a reason for a person's being unpleasant, isn't there? I thought you were too—self-conscious. You were like a master of ceremonies. You know what I mean."

Bill beckoned to a waiter. "My God! I hope you won't go spreading that."

"I didn't know you were an actor. That explains . . ."

He interrupted to order a *torta capricciosa* and two plates. "I found it by accident. It's everything, frozen. Maraschino, pistachio, nuts, rolled chocolate. . . . You ought to know now—I'm crazy about ice cream."

Celia nodded. "I see. I thought maybe you were just being unbelievably wholesome for my sake."

"Not a bit. Now if we went down to Harry's bar for old fashioneds *that* would be wholesome." He grinned. "But we sneak up back alleys for a *torta capricciosa* which, aside from other things, is an aphrodisiac. I said *a torta*. We'll share one. I haven't been paid this week."

Celia touched the clasp of her purse, then decided against it. "Anyway, it's a little cold," she said, wrapping the skirt of her coat around her legs.

"Exactly. The bar's run by an Austrian. The minute you can force a spoon between your frozen fingers he puts his tables out and beats up a batch of ice cream. Some people feel that way about it. In New York I like Howard Johnson's for *real* dissipation. Though, if you want a pure experience you should go to Schrafft's for a plain vanilla with marshmallow sauce—or a hot fudge sundae with chocolate cream. Then there's Giolitti's in Rome, Demel's in Vienna and I've heard that in Athens . . ."

She laughed. "It's funny to think of the Greeks and the Romans eating ice cream."

"It is not. No really decadent civilization can get along without it."

"Perhaps. But somehow you're not the type. You look much too sinister." She paused, embarrassed.

"Sinister?"

"Of course I understand now," she said, quickly. "You're an actor. I mean you're an actor who plays those parts."

"Not any more. I used to be. This picture was made four years ago—grade C horse opera."

"Well you *should* be. I watched you at dinner and . . ."

The waiter brought the ice cream. He didn't seem to mind furnishing the extra plate.

Bill smiled. "Yes, I saw you."

"Did you know about them all along?"

"Know what?" He divided the *torta* in equal portions and put one on her plate.

"That they were after Mr. Fox's money? That they didn't care for him at all?"

"If you had no trouble guessing, why should I?"

"Does Mr. Fox know?"

"He's an old man."

"I *hope* he doesn't. It would hurt him so much." She took a bite of the ice cream and held it in her mouth like a hot coal. "At least I think it would. Would it?"

He leaned toward her. "I'd like to ask you a question now. Then I want to forget about the whole business this evening, if you don't mind."

"I don't mind. What are these?" She pointed to some white grains, about twice the size of cooked rice.

"Pine nuts. That's the aphrodisiac. How long have you worked for Mrs. Sheridan?"

"Only six months. It seems longer."

"Has she ever mentioned Mr. Fox before? I mean, before she received his letter?"

"No. She never speaks of men—unless they're servants, but that's different."

"She's never talked of a husband?"

Celia shaved off another mouthful. "With some women Mrs. is an honorary title. Like Kentucky Colonel."

"You don't like her?"

"That isn't fair. I've got a job. So have you." She stared at him. "At least I *think* you have. You're not my idea of a private secretary."

"You're not much of a lady's companion either—now. How'd the old tiger let you go?"

"She's asleep. I gave her a pill."

"Isn't that unethical?"

"Oh no. She always has one. She even makes me wake her for another in the middle of the night. She always wants to be sure . . ."

"You mean she's sleep-nutty?"

"Yes."

"That's what I wanted to know—*is* she nutty? Do you

think she's telling the truth? I mean about being the old man's wife?"

"I don't see what would be the sense of lying. Surely Mr. Fox would . . ."

Bill nodded quickly. "Uh-huh. I just didn't want to bother the old man if she turned out to be hysterical."

"I'm sure she isn't." Celia looked across the tables. The child had gone to sleep in its mother's arms.

"Do you think she's capable of going ahead with it? If she claimed common-law marriage there'd be a lot of bad publicity."

"I doubt if that would bother her very much. What difference does it make, anyway? Somebody's got to inherit the money. It might as well be her. The others are just as bad. Besides, she hasn't any heirs herself. It just means a delay of a few years before the estate becomes public." Celia glanced again at the sleeping child.

"I suppose you're right. But the old man wouldn't like it a bit. When he goes, he'd like to go a bachelor—what's the matter? Do you know her?" He looked to the other table.

"No—I just wondered why she kept her child up so late and why she was feeding it coffee."

"That's because Italians treat children like children. Babies *want* to stay up late and they're crazy about coffee. That's why so many kids are born here. It's their favorite country."

She looked at the sky. "Maybe the moon has something to do with it, too."

Later, when Bill had finished his own ice cream and half of hers, they left the tables and took a winding street to the right which brought them to a canal. It was like those dim streets near the business district of any large city, on which trucks rumble all night. A barge floated by, bearing crates of bottled milk. A warehouse opposite was open at the water level and workmen were piling cases of red soda on the landing. A gondola, long retired from the tourist trade, moved slowly into the heart of the city with a load of artichokes.

"Are you?" she said.

"I suppose I should know what you're talking about."

They followed the concrete bank. "Are you a private secretary? Or is there something else?"

Bill took her arm. "Listen—do you have any money besides what you get from the old lady?"

"No."

"And if somebody asked you if you were really a lady's companion, what would you say?"

"I'd say yes, I was—for the moment."

"That's my answer. Four years ago, in Hollywood, I averaged about six thousand a year playing horse operas. A few months' pay and the rest of the time in casting offices. Later, I did stock and got my living and enough to buy a few clothes. Still later, in New York, I did nothing and got nothing for doing it. I started going to cocktail parties for the *food*—and at night a tribe of East Side, furnished-room bedbugs took it back again . . ."

"You probably didn't have to live like that, you know. I'm sure there was some work you could have done." They came to a tiny bridge, arched high over the water.

"Of course there was. That's what I'm trying to tell you. I had three years of law school. That should have qualified me for something—I don't know what. But the point is that I thought I was an actor. Well, I *was*, you know. A pretty good one. Also, I must admit I was thinking of money. The poorer you get the more you put your hopes on a killing. Then I was offered a job here in Italy, doing a picture. On the strength of that I borrowed enough for a third class ticket . . ."

He guided her up the stairs. She heard someone singing far down the canal.

". . . but when I got here the producer was in jail. He forgot he needed a little money to go with his credit. I traveled around Europe with a second-rate variety show until that gave out, and then started looking around again for invitations to cocktail parties. So I got disgusted with myself. I decided that this time I wasn't an actor . . . I was whatever anyone paid me to be. Above all, I was out to make money."

They had reached the top of the bridge. The black water below reflected the full moon. They stopped. "And do you think you will?" Celia said.

"I *know* I will." His eyes were the color of the water. A great scow filled with ashes drifted below them.

The movie was showing in a neighborhood theatre not much different from its counterpart in any large city. It was too poor to have more than a stub of a marquee and a flickering neon light read, ARIST N. The "O" had died. The only thing unusual about it was that it was set into the side of a graceful old palace, like a cyst on a baroque nude. To the right of the marquee was a pharmacy, at the left an *espresso* bar.

Bill directed her into the lobby, made even more shabby by the aid of powder-white fluorescent lamps on the ceiling. He bought tickets, which Celia noticed were made of paper, not cardboard, and took her to a billboard, flanked by two sickly potted plants. Below a gaudy scene of men firing pistols at each other she saw the title, *I fuorilegge di Powder Creek*. "The Outlaws of Powder Creek," he said. "You won't understand a word of it because it's been dubbed. But the good thing about my pictures is that everyone over eight years old knows exactly what's going to happen before they buy their tickets."

One of the men in the battle was wearing a star on his shirt and his face was twisted in a vaguely familiar sneer as blood dripped from his useless left arm. "That's me," Bill said, cheerfully. "Bat Saunders—a hired gunman the mine owner has brought into Powder Creek to drive out the O'Learys." He pointed to the other figures. "That's Jim O'Leary, his kid brother Jeff, and Miss Lucy Tucker, the mine owner's daughter. She's secretly engaged to Jim but has fallen for Jeff. I'm crazy about her, too, in my own twisted way. I get myself made sheriff—there's the gimmick—and I . . ." He took her arm and led her toward a curtained door. "Let's go in. See for yourself what a skunk I am."

The lights were on inside. The straight wooden seats and the curtain over the screen advertising a soft drink, reminded Celia of the movies she had seen when she was a child. The same young boys were sitting at the front (except, of course, that they would not have been up so late at home) and the same passive older folk whispered together at the back. Here and there islands of girls giggled as young men threw balls of paper and other loving missiles at them. A man with a tray suspended from his neck walked between the aisles, selling fruit and candy. Some of the boys beneath the screen began to stamp their feet. It was difficult to remember that they were little gondoliers—some of them, at least. Descendants of the republic of Venice fidgeting for the blaze of six-guns. She noticed, also, the familiar odor of cheap sweets and adolescent perspiration. She felt at home.

"Why does the mine owner want to get rid of the O'Learys?" she said. The lights began to dim and the seats screeched a final protest to slouching bodies.

"Because he's cheated them out of their claim, of course. He says he bought it from their father and has a false bill of sale to prove it. Old man O'Leary died in a mysterious mine cave-in. I was responsible for that. But Miss Lucy . . ."

A young couple sitting to their right shushed them. Stirring music filled the auditorium and a picture of Michelangelo's *David* flashed on the screen, introducing a newsreel.

Bill was right. The language was unimportant. Even the newsreel with its sports roundup, fashion parade, comic scene featuring a man with a trick cigarette holder, and its tragic view of smoking airplane wreckage accompanied by a standard dirge, was as familiar to her as the taste of popcorn. When *I fuorilegge di Powder Creek* came on she was already caught, with the rest of the audience, in that dreamlike state of belief which defies the worst movies and makes the best superfluous. Also, she began to be fascinated by Bat Saunders; and not merely because the man who played him was sitting at her side. She had no particular feelings about Mr. William Fieramosca, though he had been pleasant so far. But this stock movie badman, striding down a familiar street lined with hitching bars, shouldering his way through grizzled prospectors she had know since childhood, was one of the most disagreeable persons she had ever seen.

It was a ridiculous situation. As the cold-eyed man cut young O'Leary across the face with the barrel of his gun he also gently held her hand. She was hardly an authority on handholders but she was grateful that Bill was neither a dripper nor a kneader. She enjoyed the friendliness of his touch. But at the same time she was watching a man, with his gestures and mannerisms, shooting down the innocent, bullying the weak and displaying a chilling contempt for all other people. It did not help her to remember that this was a silly story for children. It was not what he did, but the *way*. His eyes and mouth became cruel too effortlessly. It was like watching someone when he thought he was alone. *This* was the real man, not the one at her side. And he frightened her.

The O'Learys themselves were innocuous, as she imagined they were intended to be—empty vessels for the gondoliers down front to fill with their own egos. And Miss Lucy Tucker was so clearly the second prize in a beauty contest that she could have played her part in a bathing suit without spoiling the illusion. The very fact that none of them but Bat Saunders was the least bit real convinced her that she was right. She wanted to pull away her hand, but because it was under his she left it there, afraid that he would guess her thoughts. The O'Leary brothers were entering a bar. Bat Saunders was waiting for them. She had seen this happen hundreds of times, sitting as she was now in a hard wooden chair, squirming with fear and pulling at a spike of her hair, a bar of sticky chocolate in one hand. Twelve—fourteen years ago? Not very long. Young Jeff O'Leary was pushed aside by his brother. He faced the sheriff's guns and . . .

Fine—Primo Tempo

. . . the lights went on, Part One was over.

Bill leaned to her. "He hasn't got a chance."

"I—I know. You're very convincing." She tried to make it sound like a compliment.

"Thanks. It was my first heavy and I was bearing down. The others were either hopeless or they'd been at it too long."

Celia searched his eyes. They were the same. And the mouth was faintly twisted in what might be a smile—but might also be anything else. Very well—he was an actor. But was he acting now? "You seem to know him very well."

"Who?"

"Bat Saunders."

He began to laugh and two girls in front turned to look at them. The candy butcher was going down the center aisle, calling his wares. Young men were twisting in their seats, waiting for the second part. "I do. He's the principal of a high school in Reno."

She stared at him in disbelief. "High school?"

He nodded. "I mean he's what I thought the principal was like when I was going to the school. I didn't like him."

The lights began to dim. "Do you mind if I leave you for a moment," he said. "I've got to make a call."

"No—I'll be all right." She didn't add that she was pleased. The auditorium was dark. She felt Bill getting up and at the same moment Bat Saunders' inexhaustible six-guns blazed in her face.

She was aware of nothing but the ridiculous drama of Powder Creek until the lights went up again. Gradually she forgot about William and she thought of Bat Saunders as simply another movie villain who would meet the end he deserved. Often she felt that she had literally gone back to her childhood and was sitting in the Colonial theater on "O" Street on Saturday afternoon. Ten cents admission before five. There was a dam about to be blown up. Sputtering fire crept down a long fuse to a load of dynamite. Men fighting on top of the dam. Miss Lucy racing for help. Men fighting. The fuse. The end was neat and satisfactory. Jeff and Miss Lucy stood on a hillside and vowed to rebuild all that had been torn down. His arm stole around her . . .

Celia felt a shoulder touch hers. She shuddered. The lights popped on.

"Some day all this land will be orange trees," Bill drawled, staring prophetically across the heads of the audience. Seats banged. Boys got up and stretched.

She hadn't noticed him come back. "Did you make your call?"

"Yes. Don't you think I make a good villain? I ought to keep in practice."

"I thought it was silly," she said. There was a sharp white line around his nostrils.

They stood. "Not at all. You're only sorry I didn't murder them all."

"No—of course not—!" She stopped. His eyes glittered.

He led her along a strange street, in the opposite direction from the way they had come. Past the houses to their right she heard water lapping stone foundations. "I don't like to retrace steps, do you? It's unlucky." He had taken her arm. She was afraid to draw it away.

"I wouldn't have thought you believed in luck," she said, slowly.

"That depends. If you're alone you have to. When you're with someone else—I mean *with*—it's not so important."

A boy strolled by, whistling the theme from *Limelight*. The moon looked as though it had been smeared between horizon and zenith by a vigorous child with yellow crayon. Celia remembered a winter night four year ago . . .

"When people are together they don't like surprises. They want to see the future. No more waiting around for chance. They make their own luck. I know gambling, for instance. Only the suckers keep playing for the thrill. A real gambler plays because he's alone against everyone and he doesn't care. If he's got someone else he makes a strike and gets out fast."

. . . She disliked the moon. There had been one that night—a pale winter face, leering at her.

They were passing a wine shop. Celia glanced into the tiny room where men were hunched over tables thumbing dirty cards. The low voice at her side continued. ". . . a man alone goes from one thing to another, watching his luck change back and forth. Maybe something this year, maybe nothing next. He doesn't mind as long as things keep changing."

She had gone to a college party with a young man whose hair was put down on his head like a sheet of plywood and who wore wads of cotton in his ears. She looked forward to the evening as though it were a physics exam. One prepared as well as possible and hoped it would be over soon.

". . . That's why I wanted to see you tonight. I'm tired of going along by myself, living on luck. If I had someone else with me I could plan."

She was wearing an old pearl clip which had belonged to her mother. It glowed at her throat, a quiet reproof to costume jewelry. It was the only valuable thing she owned. Her dress was poor, her bag was the wrong color. The forget-me-not corsage—which she had bought for herself, explaining to her escort that gardenias gave her a headache—seemed merely inexpensive, not original. But the pin was right—a magic emblem . . .

They turned right toward the canal. Bill was still speaking. "Don't misunderstand. It doesn't make any difference to me one way or the other—yet. What I mean is that I like you. Well, something not quite as flat as that, maybe. I know a great deal about you. You'd be surprised . . ."

She had been asked to dance by a young man who looked like Gregory Peck. Celia grimaced. Why did lonely people have fan-magazine dreams in spite of themselves? They might pretend to be above that sort of thing but they were more childishly romantic than anyone else. For all she knew, the boy with the plywood hair and the cotton in his ears—who had deserted her for the punch bowl—was someone she would have enjoyed knowing, if she had only tried. While the other . . .

In a doorway she saw a man and a woman pressed together. As she passed they moved back and a ray of moonlight struck their faces. The woman's mouth was swollen and numb with kisses.

. . . Gregory Peck. She had noticed a tiny spot of congealed blood on the inner edge of his ear. It made him seem violent and adventurous—though of course he had only cut himself shaving. He spoke with callow sophistication. That consisted mostly of making jokes about virgins. Nevertheless she was impressed. Not by what he said but by his assurance. She tried to respond in the same manner but she overdid it. Once or twice he raised a quizzical eyebrow (always the left one).

"Are you listening to me?"

"Of course," Celia said. They were approaching the canal.

"I don't believe you. I said, let's take a gondola home."

"All right. If you wish." There were a group of men standing under a light beside the canal. One of them was wearing a wide straw hat shoved back on his head.

"There's an old friend of mine." Bill guided her toward the group. "He used to take care of the boats in Central Park."

Celia let herself be drawn forward. She didn't want to be taken "home," or taken anywhere. But she gave in to the pressure of Bill's hand on her arm. The moon silvered the water.

. . . He asked her to leave with him. *My Caddy's outside.* It took her a moment to realize that he was speaking of a make of automobile. She decided he was a little younger than he had admitted. *At least there will be plenty of room,* she said, smiling. His hand clutched her back and pulled her body close. She had meant, literally, that it was a big car—nothing else. *You're a swell gal. A man gets plenty sick of these little refrigerators.* Her stomach was beginning to feel strange. She had not meant so much—nor so little. *Come on, let's get out of this den of lambs.* She'd thought that rather funny. But she didn't really want . . .

"Come on," Bill said. The man in the straw hat was leading them down to his gondola, which was moored beside a shallow flight of stone steps. "You realize you can't walk home from a boat ride?" He looked her severely in the eye.

Celia nodded and allowed him to help her to one of the red cushioned seats.

"You're lucky to find me," the gondolier said, in an accent which reminded Celia of New York. "I don't usually work this late." They began to move into the canal.

Bill took her hand.

"It's my niece. She's havin' a kid. *You* get a midwife in the house once an' see what I mean."

Celia felt Bill's arm on her shoulder . . .

. . . It happened as predictably as a dirty joke. The car soon grew warm under the breath of the heater. The moon was a slice of lemon. She hadn't minded when the young man stopped and turned to her with heroic features gone slack. This was to be expected. She might have enjoyed it, almost, if there had been anything honest in his fumbling embrace. But as she was struggling to get her breath it struck her that *he* thought it was wrong. Far from wishing to make love to her, he seemed to want to punish her. His fingers cut into her arms, her lips were bruised against her teeth. She pushed him away, slightly, still ready to make allowances. After all, he was male. She supposed that made it different. But he was furious and forced her to him again, as though her resistance were a personal insult. At last she began struggling in real terror, not only because she was afraid of being bodily hurt, but because she was humiliated. The more she fought the more ferocious he became. Her left arm was badly wrenched and there was a taste of blood in her mouth. At last a voice deep within her ordered her to stop . . . simply let go. If she did not she would be injured. She also knew that the only way to preserve the crumbling defenses of her mind was to give way and accept whatever happened. By retreating she won the biggest part of the battle—herself. After that it was a dreamlike encounter with a stranger who could not hurt her. She watched the moon through the windowshield. Printed in the glass in white letters she saw the words, ᗡ⅂ƎIHS-ƎℲ∀S. Then the young man drove her home. She noticed that his lips were quivering and, once, a pair of childish tears rolled down his cheeks. She left his car without speaking and walked through the bitter night to the door of her rooming house, trying to hold her arm to her breast so that it wouldn't pain. When she undressed for bed she found that her clip was missing. She never saw it again.

Suddenly she felt Bill's arm tighten. They were in the shadow of a tall house, drifting in the silent canal. Water slapped at the floor of the gondola. He drew her toward him. She turned and stared at his face as though it were on a distant screen. Slowly his hand relaxed and allowed her to draw back. His smile might have been comforting if it had not been so knowing. She turned her head and stared into the water. Bill began to ask the gondolier about his family. There were eight, the man answered. Nine now, probably. They lived in three rooms. "All right, in New York that's a lot of people in three rooms. Here it's more like your family. If too many of them goes you get lonesome, I swear."

In a short while they arrived at the landing of Mr. Fox's house. Celia got out and waited for Bill to open the door. She was angry with herself for losing her head. She had always sworn that she wouldn't let it make any difference—that time—if . . . She heard the jingle of silver coins. The gondolier said, "Good night, lady," and she saw the high prow of the boat turn toward the center of the canal. Bill came up beside her, searching his pockets for keys.

"Some day you may get tired of playing it alone." His voice was pleasantly casual.

"People can't always choose what they do," she answered.

"That's no excuse for *never* choosing." He opened the door.

She didn't look at him. "I—I had a nice evening."

He took her hand and she glanced up. "Some day when we're rich we'll buy up every movie I was ever in and sit around showing them over and over while I eat barrels of ice cream." He was grinning.

"That will be very nice," she said.

"Or we might buy this house. I suppose it'll be vacant—soon. We might as well." He stood aside as she walked in.

There was a long whistle from a boat far out in the lagoon.

"We might enjoy it here, you know," he continued. "But of course we'd have to be partners." He closed the door softly.

Celia went directly to bed, setting her traveling clock to ring at three. It was obviously unnecessary to give the old lady her second tablet, but if she were to remember that she had been deprived she would claim not to have slept a wink all night. Celia put the clock under her pillow and fell into an uneasy nap from which she woke by herself at ten minutes to three. She went into the old lady's room.

She had never seen Mrs. Sheridan's face so handsome. All of the small marks had been wiped from it, as a receding sea leaves a beach. Only the large lines, made by time itself, were left. The features had become proud without being vain. The lips had forgotten cruelty. The closed eyelids looked as though they had been carved of marble. After the first slight shock, like stepping from a warm room into a bitter starlit winter evening, Celia knew she was in the presence of Death. She took the woman's hand. A chill was setting in, and nothing in the world could warm her again. The girl went to one side of the room, brought a chair back to the bedside and sat beside the corpse in the dim light. From time to time she brushed imaginary specks of dirt from the edge of the sheet, as she offered reverence to the spirit of the old woman.

A quarter of an hour later Celia got up and turned on the light. The first thing she saw was the water glass, empty and uncovered. That was strange because Mrs. Sheridan would never have taken a drink by herself. She would have called her companion to give it to her. And if she had called and found no one, she would never have gone back to bed. Then, on the other side of the lamp, she saw a bottle. It was empty but she could see that it was the one which had contained the sugar pills. To make sure she checked the old lady's handbag, standing where she had left it on the chair. There was no doubt. It was the same.

Why? Why should a woman who was well only a few hours ago and feeling even oppressively normal, be lying dead beside an empty bottle of absolutely harmless pills? Celia stared at the white face. It was less beautiful in the bright light. She went to the door and switched the room into darkness.

Mrs. Sheridan had been murdered.

CHAPTER NINE

"Dead!" Mr. Fox flopped over in bed like a beached fish. "Can't you think of a better way to wake a man?"

"Effective, isn't it? She'd be just as dead, however, if I woke you with harp music and cologne on your temples."

"I believe you mean it." Cecil opened and shut his mouth several times, savoring the night juices.

"Mrs. Sheridan ceased to live last evening, probably shortly after she went to bed." William's voice was cold. He walked to a window and pushed open the shutters. From the house's eaves came the optimistic, early-morning chatter of birds. A street cleaner's hose played water on the cobbles in the square. The young man turned back to his employer. "I learned about it an hour ago."

Cecil looked at his watch. "Thank God you didn't tell me *then*. I haven't been up this early since I was young enough to be up this late."

"Her companion found the old lady at three o'clock." He came to Mr. Fox's bedside. An hourglass stood on the floor, within reach of the bed.

Mr. Fox stretched his muscular arms. "The trouble with elaborate pleasures . . ." He stopped and yawned.

". . . pleasures, is that too many flies get in the works.
"Ointment," William corrected. "I don't want to blubber with sentimentality, but the woman *is* dead. You aren't a little curious?"

"You forget that I'm too old to get a vicarious thrill out of dying. If you want to know the truth, I'm glad to hear I outstayed her. What was it, blood pressure? She always ran to it." He threw back the covers and stared down at his pink toes.

"Sleeping pills. A whole bottle of them."

The old man's eyes opened wide. He sat on the edge of the bed. "Not suicide! I don't believe it."

William shook his head. "No—neither do I."

Cecil stood up and shuffled his feet into slippers. "Hand me my robe, will you? I don't suppose you thought to tell Massimo to have my breakfast sent up." He took the robe, draped it over his shoulders like a cape and walked to the window.

"It's coming."

The old man stared into the square. "It's enough to make you join a church."

"What is?"

"Oh—death. Very sobering." His voice was hushed and mellifluous.

"I wouldn't," said William, quietly. "People who join churches late in life never do it because *they* want to but because they think other people should."

Cecil turned around. "How do *you* think she died?"

"It could have been an accident."

Fox scratched the fringe of hair above his ears. "I suppose. She always did take sleeping medicine."

"Or it might have been done on purpose."

"Damn. Damn it to hell!"

The young man gazed at him steadily. "It's a little late to show concern."

Cecil grinned. "A little more of your sanctimony will ruin my breakfast, boy. Keep it up and I'll have to tell you to ride your saddle out of here." He went to the door of the dumb-waiter and pushed the button impatiently. "Now tell me something I need to know," he said, going back to his bed and throwing himself down.

"That is why I am here," William said, keeping his voice even.

"You went out with her companion—this Johns girl—last night, is that right?"

"Yes."

"When did you come back?"

"About one."

"You said the girl found the body at three?"

William sat down. "That is what she told me."

"Then why did you only know about it an hour ago? Not that I blame you for keeping it to yourself. Another hour or two wouldn't have done any harm, you know."

"I'm afraid you're wrong about that. We'll have to report the death. That's why I wanted to talk to you before the police get here."

"You called them?" Cecil was alarmed.

"Not yet. There are certain things we have to settle. Let me go on."

"Who's stopping you?"

"The girl didn't tell me until this morning. The cook found her in the kitchen at five o'clock, drinking tea and writing a letter. She half scared him to death. He ran up and told me."

A buzzer sounded at the dumb-waiter door. The old man looked annoyed. "Where the hell's the help around here?"

William stood. "I told Massimo not to come up. I'll get it—we don't have much time."

"You're damn right you'll get it. I put that machine in there to get my food up hot, not to save work."

The young man went to the door in the wall and took out a well-laden silver tray. "I got dressed as quickly as I could and hurried down to the kitchen. I had a feeling . . ."

"Oh Lord, boy. Do you ever have a feeling that your best wine is turning or that a good looking pear is mush? No, not once. But birth and death—pshaw! Anyone can have a feeling about them."

William placed the tray on a bed table which stood along the wall at the right side of the bed. The muscles of his jaw twitched. "Anyway, I hurried to the kitchen."

"You said she was writing a letter."

"I'm coming to that." William wheeled the table over to the bed, shoving the free end across the old man's belly. He removed the covers from the dishes. There were a thick slice of browned ham, six fried eggs, a half loaf of French bread oozing butter, a quart pitcher of orange juice, some plain *fior di latte* cheese sprinkled heavily with pepper, a small, chilled bottle of kirsch, and coffee.

"It took me ten years to teach them how to do this. Nothing in the world like breakfast. I don't suppose you had any."

"No," William said, swallowing. "I said we haven't got much time. If we wait too long it will seem suspicious. I wish you'd let me go on."

"Sure—go ahead." Cecil cut into the ham. "Don't move that . . ."

The young man had leaned down to take up the hourglass, which was in danger of being kicked over.

"Just turn it upside down. I like to see it run."

William picked up the object and looked at it closely. "Yellow sand?"

Mr. Fox nodded. "Present from Voltor. Pretty, isn't it? It runs less than an hour, though," he added, sadly. "Now then—you got to the kitchen. The girl was writing a letter."

"She told me Mrs. Sheridan was dead. Last night, she said, she got up to give the old lady her second sleeping pill . . ."

"Second?"

"Yes. According to the girl her employer always took two. One before she went to sleep and one in the middle of the night. The bottle was left on the night-table. When she got up to give her the second pill all of them were gone and the old lady was stone dead."

Mr. Fox broke off a chunk of hot bread. "She had been dead for some time?"

"Yes. The body was already losing temperature. There was no question of reviving her. So she went down to the kitchen to wait until somebody was up. It didn't occur to her to wake anyone. She's almost as matter-of-fact about people dying as you are."

"Very sensible girl. Why the kitchen?"

"She said she wanted some tea—and that the first person to get up would probably come to the kitchen anyway."

Cecil nodded, poured himself a large glass of orange juice and a shot of kirsch. "And the letter?"

"She was writing to herself." William strolled across the room to examine the clock on the mantel.

The old man looked up. "Herself?"

"Yes. She says she often writes letters to herself. I mean letters, not a diary. The kind you stamp and mail. It would give me the creeps."

"I don't see why. You talk to yourself, don't you?"

"Yes. Though I hardly think I'd call myself on the telephone." He touched the clock. "This is from the old woman, isn't it?"

"Uh-huh. Her first bad investment."

"How'd she get her money?" William caressed Pierrette with his little finger.

The old man sponged a fistful of bread in egg yolk. "From me."

"Then it's true what she said." He turned and looked squarely at Mr. Fox.

"What did she say?" The old man's voice was casual.

"That you lived together, long ago, as man and wife."

Cecil smiled. With his mouth full he looked like a boy caught robbing a candy case. He chewed. "Don't judge harshly, boy. You should have seen her once."

"She had no money of her own?"

"Just a simple small-town girl with the combined charms of Venus and the giant squid. I put up with her for six months. I really was going to marry her, in the beginning, but some native cunning saved me. She had nothing to complain about. I gave her a stack and she's been adding to it ever since."

"Native cunning," William said, coming back to his employer's bedside, "is just about the definition of common law. Usage given the force of statute. She said you called yourself Sheridan then. How come?"

"That's my legal name. Fox is my mother's; I've always liked it better."

"If Mrs. Sheridan were alive now she would have herself declared your wife."

Cecil snickered. "I'd as soon be married to a Vovv."

"What's a Vovv?"

"Women who live on the fifth moon of Jupiter. They spend the afternoon getting their mandibles polished and their snakes set; then visit each other at five for little cups of blood and man-sandwiches. You didn't bring my book back."

"I have it in my room. Do you know anything about common law, Mr. Fox?"

"Not much. It sounds like one of those things people assure you are perfectly respectable without believing it for a minute, like a case of crabs."

"As it applies to marriage in certain of the United States you have only to live with someone of the other sex 'openly and notoriously' as man and wife and you're married, whether you get a license or not. The amount of time doesn't matter, either."

Cecil pushed his table away, slowly. "Good Lord! I'm a bigamist!"

William grinned. "Maybe. Last night, at dinner, Mrs. Sheridan announced that she was ready to stake her claim. Of course it would mean some notoriety for her. In the beginning, when she arrived, I believe she hadn't thought it necessary. But when she saw her competition . . ."

Cecil wiped his mouth and took another drink of kirsch. "What good would it do her? If I *were* going to die I'd simply have disinherited her."

The young man drew the table back to its place on the

wall and picked up the tray. "First of all, as your wife and only living relative, she would have a very good chance at the money. A common-law marriage is just as valid as any other when it comes to inheritance. If she couldn't have got the money she would at least be able to tie it up, for a long, long time. But that isn't the important question now . . ."

Cecil's eyes twinkled. "Yes, I see. The fact is I'm not going to die—yet. Therefore I would simply find myself married—to the Queen of all the Vovvs. You're wondering if I was standing behind the serving door or listening down the drain. If I did, maybe I also helped the old bag take her medicine last night. Is that it?"

William carried the tray to the dumb-waiter, shoved it on to one of the huge shelves and pushed the button. "Maybe you did."

"And maybe I didn't!" the old man snapped.

He closed the door and turned back to the bed. "I'm merely showing you what might happen if someone found out you weren't a helpless invalid. The guests can't speak to the servants, but the police could."

Cecil nodded. "You're right. I'll talk to Massimo."

"Another possibility—assuming the death was more than an accident—is that one of your other two guests got to her."

"What a pretty thought."

"They had every reason to think she was going to walk off with the spoils. Each one of them has already invested time and . . ." He looked down at the hourglass. ". . . money in you."

Mr. Fox looked fretfully at his wrist watch. "I'm disappointed in Sims. At the top this couldn't be worth more than fifteen hundred. He has a small soul."

"And if I know you they're going to invest more."

The old man looked up blandly. "Heavens to gracious —you misjudge me."

William ignored him. "So, if it wasn't an accident, they both have very strong motives for killing her."

Mr. Fox reached for a cigar in the bedtable cabinet. "Why assume it wasn't?"

William smiled. "When you take care of the worst, the best takes care of itself. If one of your guests became a suspect, the story of your little joke would probably come out anyway. After all, the police are not going to be so blinded by your money as the potential heirs. They might even have done a little reading. I believe a fairly complete collection of Elizabethan plays is available in Italian."

Cecil heaved himself up. He sat silently on the edge of the bed, pulling clouds of smoke from his cigar. At last he turned to his secretary. "So you know."

"How could I help it? Any actor would give twenty years of his life to play the part you've given me. You must have known that."

"I'd have been just as happy if you hadn't guessed. I thought if I told you what it was you'd ham it. Anyway, it should be perfectly clear now that I wouldn't harm a a hair on her chin. Damn it, boy—she's ruined the show! I don't know if you're not to blame. You shouldn't have gone out last night. You're one hell of a stage manager."

"I wanted to ask the girl if she thought the old woman was bluffing. I assumed you would want to know if you were married or not."

"Humph!" Mr. Fox stood up. "Fix me a drink. I'm going to take a bath."

William spoke slowly, like a professor giving a lesson. "The important thing is for you to keep the police from investigating anything more than a simple accident. You've lived here a long time. You must have some influence."

The old man rubbed his bristling chin. "I have a little. I've spent enough money here."

"Good. Report the woman's death and emphasize that you want as little fuss as possible. That way they'll give it only a routine check." William went to the dumbwaiter and opened the door. The ropes were slapping against the wall of the shaft. He waited.

Mr. Fox picked up his robe. "Then you *don't* think it was an accident?"

"As a matter of fact I do. I'm just taking care of the worst, as I said."

"And the girl? What does she think?"

William smiled. "Leave Miss Johns to me, sir."

Cecil went to the bathroom door. He turned, scratching the stomach of his gaudy pajamas. "It's too bad to give up the entertainment."

The young man shrugged. "Why give it up?"

"Well, the police are going to clutter the scenery."

"Only for awhile. When they're gone you can bring up the last act curtain."

Mr. Fox nodded. "I hoped you would say that. What's the phrase—don't give up the show?"

"Ship."

Cecil nodded. "Bring the drink, the phone, and the washable cards. I'll call from the tub and we can have a hand before the *carabinieri* come. Quarter ante, all right?"

The cage appeared in the open doorway, loaded with ice cubes and a fresh bottle of bourbon. "You haven't paid me yet, remember?"

The old man tried to look absent-minded. "Dear, dear. Is it a week yet? How the days fly by."

"None fly so quickly that I don't count them."

Mr. Fox released a large, hurt sigh and went into the bathroom. William removed the bottle and the ice from the dumb-waiter and fixed his employer a thumping drink.

CHAPTER TEN

After breakfast, the morning Mrs. Sheridan's death was discovered, Anson Sims was seated on his bed cutting his toenails when there came a knock on his door. He was expecting it.

Henry Voltor stuck his head in and when he saw Anson he entered and shut the door tightly. "Well?"

Anson did the little toe of his left foot before he looked up. "Well?"

"You know, of course."

"You mean her death?"

"Yes."

"I know," Anson said, brushing a pile of clippings together on the bed cover.

Henry began to smile. "I had no idea you would act so quickly. Maybe it was for the best, after all."

Sims stood up, shuffled into his ancient slippers and took a folded envelope from his shirt pocket. "You must be the judge of that."

"I hope you were careful."

"I beg your pardon?" He opened the envelope and began placing the discarded toenails inside.

"I said I hope you were careful." Henry's voice was sharp.

"Are you trying to pretend to *me?*"

"What on earth do you mean, pretend?"

"That you are not responsible for what happened last

night." Anson folded the paper and put it back in his shirt pocket.

Henry's face grew flushed. "That's a lie!"

"Do you deny you told me yesterday afternoon that you would find the first opportunity to . . ." He looked quickly around the room. ". . . that this would happen?"

"*I* told you? You were the one who suggested it. I merely told you the story of a case I had heard. The rest was your idea."

"It was *not*."

"It was."

Both men faced each other with the helpless anger of the old, whose battles must be fought with shaking voices.

"That is a barefaced lie!"

Suddenly Henry turned away and went to the door. He opened it, looked out and then turned around, pushing the door shut with his back. "We must be more careful. The police will be here in a moment."

"But I will not have you intimating . . ."

Voltor held up one hand. "Please. We mustn't argue. What about 'trust'? After all, we agreed to work together."

Anson calmed. "Together. Yes."

"You naturally do not want to admit to anything openly. I quite understand that. I . . ."

"I'm admitting to nothing because I've *done* nothing. Is that clear?" Sims stood before his bed with his legs spread and part of his shirttail out.

Henry was icy. "Very well. You've done nothing."

"That's right. Nothing."

"Let us return to the case of the nephews. I *assume* you remember it?"

"Yes."

"Very well. Suspicion fell on one of them. The other provided him with an alibi. The police could not break it and at last turned their investigation upon the footman—or it may have been one of the valets, I'm not exactly . . ."

"And you wish me to give you such an alibi?"

Voltor forced a sour smile. "You will remember that we are still speaking of the nephews. We don't *know* that either was guilty. The old aunt may have slipped down the service stairs by herself. Or the man who was hanged for the crime might have been guilty, to give British justice its due."

Sims glared at the smaller man. He was suspicious of loquacity.

"The important thing for the nephews was *not* to know how the murder had been done or who had done it. They were concerned with only one thing—covering each other. Is that clear?"

Anson shook his head. "Why was it better not to know? I should think they would have to."

Henry faced his accomplice. "First, because it sweetened their consciences. Each thought that the man he was protecting might *not* be a murderer after all. And the better the conscience the clearer the eye. Don't you agree?"

"Ah—yes. Indeed I do." Anson shifted his gaze.

"Second and most important, it helped strengthen their trust."

"Trust?"

"Frightfully important, trust. Neither was quite so tempted to supply the details of the crime to the police. We must assume that they had agreed to inherit equally." Henry stared intently at his companion.

"Hmmm? Oh yes. Oh dear yes. I understand." Anson had suddenly grown more friendly, like a deacon after service.

"You see how ignorance helped them? First, it strengthened their alibi—by the way, I'm sure they used a very simple one. Second, it increased their faith in each other by reducing those factors which may have endangered it."

Sims went to his dresser. He was smiling. "You've forgotten one thing." He opened a drawer and took out a pair of rolled black socks.

"What is that?"

"If either of them *were* guilty, the other felt safer . . ." Anson shook out the socks and brought them back to the bed. "Knowing that his own life was in no danger as long as he was needed to supply the murderer with an alibi." He sat down and inserted a slender white foot in the mouth of a stocking.

Henry studied the bony shoulders straining at the cloth of Anson's shirt. "That might be the biggest advantage of all," he said, slowly.

Sims reached under the bed for his shoes. "Exactly. They had to help each other. Above all, they had to keep quiet."

"That hardly needs to be said."

Anson picked one shoe up and held it between his knees. "Tell it not in Gath . . ." He began to retie a broken shoestring. "Publish it not in the streets of Askelon."

Henry wiped the back of his fragile neck with a large white handkerchief. "Quite."

CHAPTER ELEVEN

Maresciallo Rizzi questioned Celia in Mrs. Sheridan's room, after the body had been removed. He was middle-aged and fatherly looking, with a great, beaked nose, a shiny bald head, amazingly delicate hands and black tufts of hair growing from his ears. He spoke precise, British English, deliberately paced, as though he were holding back his own thoughts to accommodate her inferior intelligence. This was less patronizing than true. Celia knew she couldn't resist him openly. If he suspected that she was withholding information he was capable of picking her mind to pieces. She *had* to mislead him, nevertheless. It would be so easy simply to tell him what she knew. But she could not condemn another person to death—even a murderer. So she used the only two weapons she had: her youth and her sex. Perhaps the *Maresciallo* was less fatherly than he looked.

She began by telling him that she had spent the last evening with Mr. Fieramosca and had not returned to the house until one o'clock.

He nodded and glanced at her figure. All was in order. "You are intimate with the young man?"

She denied it indignantly until she saw his heavy eyebrows gather in a frown. Perhaps all was *not* in order. Celia managed to blush with disturbing ease. They hadn't known each other long, she said. Only a few hours, in fact. She had agreed to spend the evening with him because . . .

Maresciallo Rizzi allowed himself a faint, off-duty smile. Things were in order, after all. Furthermore, a girl of reasonably good family. "And your employer had given you permission to leave?"

Celia saw her chance. She drew a tiny handkerchief from her pocket and gently blew her nose. She shook her head. No, she had gone without permission. There was a moon. Venice seemed *such* a beautiful city.

His face remained stern, but the eyes were now full of sympathy. *Quite* in order. The young have only a few years . . . He passed a hand across his pate, regretfully. The gesture spoke of Signora Rizzi, increased responsibilities and limited opportunities.

Celia told him how she had prepared the old woman for bed, how she had given her a sleeping pill and left the bottle in her bag, as she had been ordered to do.

His eyes grew sharp, but not unfriendly. "Perhaps you gave her the sleeping pill to make sure you would be free for the evening?"

She looked shocked. Of course not.

He nodded. "Nevertheless, you were not displeased to give her the drug last night, were you?"

She hesitated. Then she affected to be honest. "I—no, I was not displeased."

He waved the confession aside. "Perfectly natural." Suddenly he leaned forward. "Why were you supposed to leave the bottle in her bag?"

"She was afraid—of waking up, I mean."

"Of nothing else?"

Celia smiled, wanly. "You'd have to know her. It was

her sleep. She would go into a panic if she didn't have the sleeping tablets within reach."

The *Maresciallo* raised his head. The huge nose seemed to twitch, like a hunting dog's. "But I understood *you* were the one who got up to give her a second pill in the middle of the night. Am I wrong?"

Celia used her handkerchief once more. "Yes—I did, every evening."

The voice was gentle. "Then why did she keep the bottle in her bag, if you brought her what she needed?"

Celia shook her head. "I've already told you. Because it was *hers*. I was supposed to get up at night and give one to her because she was paying me. If she wanted a handkerchief she would call me for that, too."

"You did not think two tablets each evening were excessive?"

Here was the danger point. She tried to sound crisp and professional. "Perhaps, but if she didn't have them she would worry herself awake. At her age the sleep did her more good than the tablets did harm."

"Obviously not." The *Maresciallo* was above easy sarcasm. "You were not fond of Mrs. Sheridan?"

She hesitated. "Not *fond*, no. But I didn't dislike her. I couldn't ever wish her dead." She blinked her eyes and real tears appeared. "If I'd been here she would be alive now . . ."

The *Maresciallo* glared at her wet cheeks. Once again he passed his hand along his head. Then he sighed. "Yes. No doubt."

He continued to circle her with questions, laying polite siege. Unless he found a vulnerable spot he would not bother to bring up his forces. If an old woman habitually took too many sleeping pills what could you expect?

Nevertheless, he was not here to prove her death was an accident, but to prove it couldn't have been anything else. His superiors had also asked him to be as unobtrusive as possible—which probably meant someone suspected suicide and wanted it hushed. Very well. It was all one to him. As long as he was sure it was nothing more. . . .

He looked at the girl. What a pity she wasn't a bit fatter. So many of these American girls were afraid of food.

He took Mrs. Sheridan's handbag from its place on the chair beside the bed and placed its contents neatly in a row on the dresser top. Notebook, wallet, compact, three hotel keys, passport, a bundle of receipted bills, a clean handkerchief, some nose drops, lavender smelling salts, and a folder of National City Bank travelers' checks.

"As far as you know," he said, "are any of her belongings missing?"

"No."

"You are sure this is the amount of money she was carrying?" He opened the wallet and fanned out a packet of fifty-dollar bills. "*dieci, undici, dodici*—six hundred dollars in United States currency and—a thousand dollars in travelers checks. Is that right?"

"Yes. Approximately. I don't know exactly what . . ." She stopped.

"Something is missing?" His voice stabbed at her.

Celia met his eyes. For the first time she realized how dangerous her position was. If she were caught lying she would be accused of the murder herself. And yet something *was* missing. She was astonished that he didn't see it. "You'll think I'm very heartless," she said, slowly.

He wouldn't allow her to look away. She felt him forcing himself into her mind. "Heartless?" he said. "Why heartless?"

"N—nothing. Except that I just remembered that tomorrow is pay day. I have a month's salary coming. It's not very much—only fifty dollars, but . . . You see, how can I think such things at a time like this?" She held her breath.

Maresciallo Rizzi continued to stare at her for a moment, then he turned deliberately back to the articles on the dresser. "That is too bad. I'm sure that if you make a claim—at the proper time—you will be paid what is due to you. You have accounts?"

"No." She clenched her hands to keep from trembling.

Suddenly he turned back. "It is not possible that there was more here? You might have taken something for yourself." His voice was light. It held no reproach.

Celia looked genuinely surprised. "Do you mean you're accusing *me* of . . ."

He didn't apologize, but his manner softened. "Very well. Once again, is there anything—anything at all—missing from this purse?"

She shook her head. "I—I don't think so. I'm sure everything's here." Her eyes were wide. She brought to them all the innocence of her childhood. Celia glanced at the contents of the purse. It was impossible that he did not notice.

The *Maresciallo* stared thoughtfully at her throat. He seemed disturbed by something. Finally, he asked her to describe what she had done after she had discovered Mrs. Sheridan's body. Celia told of going downstairs to the kitchen to make herself tea. She had waited for the household to awake.

"You realize that you should have reported the death immediately?"

"Why? She had been dead for some time. There was no hope of reviving her."

He shrugged. "The next time, Miss Johns, you will be less considerate of other people's sleep . . . including my own . . . in the interest of public order."

"I'm very sorry."

"You should be. Could your employer have committed suicide, do you believe?"

"Oh, no. I'm sure she did not."

"You are sure? Or are you trying to cover up."

"I am sure," she said, firmly.

"Then how do you believe she died?"

"It must have been an accident, don't you think?"

He pulled at an earlobe. "I'm asking you what you think, Miss Johns. Do you mean by 'accident' that she woke up, took one or several of the pills and then, confused by the drug, proceeded to take the rest?"

Celia nodded. "Something like that. Because I wasn't here . . ."

"Yes—you were out with your friend. I shall speak to him. You do not mind?"

"No, of course not."

He shook his head. "The young men these days are not what they were before the war, I believe."

"I'm not sure that I understand."

He frowned. "Less—ah—thoughtful. You are interested in Venice?" He was watching her hair.

"Oh yes. I think it's extremely beautiful."

"Perhaps you would honor me by . . ."

"Yes?" In profile his face seemed familiar . . . The portrait of an ancient Doge, faintly embarrassed.

"Nothing. I have nothing more to ask—today."

She felt a thrill of power. So *this* was how it was done. It was like getting a tender glance from an eagle. "If I can help in any way . . ."

Maresciallo Rizzi had resumed his official air. A man of responsibilities—and Signora Rizzi. "It is your opinion, then, that Mrs. Sheridan died by accident?"

"Yes." It was too late to back out. Now she was not only protecting a murderer, she was protecting herself . . .

When he left, Celia went into her own room and locked the door which had connected her to Mrs. Sheridan. She had refused to change rooms. Death was like lightning; it was not dangerous before or after it struck. She went to her window and stared out at the mimosa tree leaning over the garden wall. Celia was almost certain that she knew who had murdered Mrs. Sheridan. Now that *Maresciallo* Rizzi was downstairs speaking to the others she could prove it. But she was afraid. Not, strangely, of the murderer, whose life she was shielding. She was only afraid of herself. As long as she had any doubt about the identity of the killer she did not have to judge herself for protecting him. But if she destroyed that doubt . . . Below, the mimosa tree stirred uneasily in the wind.

Celia turned and walked quickly from her room to the elevator. She rode up one floor and went directly to William's room. He had told her it was at the left hand corner of the house. She entered without knocking.

Ten minutes later she was satisfied that William had been in Mrs. Sheridan's room sometime yesterday evening. Of course that was not "proof." For instance, she didn't know *why* he had murdered the old woman. She decided to say nothing to the police, at least until she knew that.

CHAPTER TWELVE

"Come in, Mr. Sims. You are very kind to give me your time."

The man came awkwardly across the study to the chair the *Maresciallo* indicated. He scowled at his trouser legs as he sat down and arranged them in a horizontal pleat on each thigh to preserve the crease at the knees. Rizzi noticed the cracked shoes. He reminded himself that wealthy Anglo-Saxons tolerate and even vaunt old clothes instead of consigning them charitably to the poor.

"I hope you will not mind if I ask you a few questions, sir?" The *Maresciallo* flashed his most "southern" smile. In dealing with foreigners it was frequently wise to appear more or less Neapolitan. Warm-hearted, childish, a charming stranger to the industrial revolution.

Anson glared at the tapestry across the room. "Very well."

Rizzi nodded. "Good. First, I understand that you and the late Mrs. Sheridan and a certain Mr. Voltor arrived here several days ago as house guests. Can you tell me the purpose of the visit?" His voice, he hoped, was sufficiently musical. He would have preferred to thicken his accent but he was afraid of overdoing it.

The old man set his lips. "I have no idea why *they* came."

The *Maresciallo* nodded respectfully. At the back of his mind he heard the clang of cracked guitars and still another encore of *Santa Lucia* from a toothless troubadour. "Very well. I see you are nothing if not precise, sir. Why did *you* come?"

The baleful eyes turned to him. "To be with an old friend who is dying."

"Ah—dying you say? You don't mean Mr. Fox? I had heard that he was very sick but I had no idea he was dying."

"He is dying," Anson said, solemnly.

"What a dreadful burden for you, sir. I understand your grief. What is more sacred than the memory of an old friend? As our poet Tasso says . . . But you said you didn't know why the others had come. Weren't they also friends of the dying man?"

Sims kept stubbornly silent.

"Naturally they came to be with him at his death?"

Again silence.

"They were friends of Mr. Fox, after all, as you are."

"Humph!" The old man shifted angrily in his chair.

Rizzi's voice grew grave. "I see you have your doubts. Of course I don't wish to interfere in what is obviously a private matter, but you can understand, I'm sure. It may have some bearing on my investigation." He hoped that he was sufficiently soothing. Who would hesitate to tell everything to a simple child of the sun? *Marechiaro! Marechiaro!* Welcome to our siren shores!

"They are *not* his friends," Anson said, sternly.

"You think they had another reason for coming?"

"Scavengers!"

"Excuse me. One of them is no longer living."

"Especially the woman," Sims said.

"And the man?" He tried to hint of a land of tears and laughter and easily forgiven sins.

Anson straightened. His long fingers twitched. "The man . . ."

"Yes?" Rizzi leaned forward, his wolfish face wreathed in borrowed sentiment.

"The man is a murderer."

The *Maresciallo* got up, slowly. The good-natured, half-comic policeman was gone. The picturesque bay of Naples faded from view. He grinned. It was the face of a hunter with a fresh kill. "Now tell me everything."

"I think . . ."

"You don't understand. I don't want your opinion. I want to know everything about this matter from the beginning. I can take you into immediate custody unless you completely satisfy me that you have told all you know."

The old man made a show of resistance.

"Quickly! The smallest lie and I will see to it that you have a view of Venice you'll never find on a post card—from the inside of a stone cell."

"But . . ."

"I said start!"

As Anson Sims began to tell of the events leading to Mrs. Sheridan's death and of Henry Voltor's open threat to murder her, *Maresciallo* Rizzi watched his lean, quivering cheeks and bony wrists. One suspected that the United States was not a rich country after all. So many of its citizens were underfed . . .

Not quite half an hour later, Henry Voltor was sitting in the chair still lukewarm from Anson's meagre haunches. He had begun the interview with a semblance of self-control, but lured on by the *Maresciallo's* orange-scented questions he too had accused his rival of murdering the old woman.

"But I've *told* you all I know. He's guilty. He said he meant to kill her and he did."

"He *said?*"

"Well—yes, I'm sure he did."

"You don't seem sure."

"I am. I know he killed her. If you take him into custody he'll confess, I know." Voltor paused, then nodded vigorously. "Yes, take him in, by all means."

Rizzi meditatively dug into one ear with his little finger. "What is the expression in English when one party goes to the police and accuses another? A single word, I believe."

Voltor frowned. "I'm sure I don't know. Look here, aren't you going to arrest him?"

"Informer." The *Maresciallo* examined a fleck of wax.

"What has that got to do with it? Don't you see? If you take him . . ."

"Yes, Mr. Voltor. I see perfectly." Rizzi fastidiously brushed his hands. "An informer can never be trusted as long as he has something to gain by the acceptance of his information. That is a fairly simple principle which a great many people, and nations, choose to forget. Now *if* I were to take Mr. Sims into custody on suspicion of murder would you gain anything, Mr. Voltor?"

"Why . . ." Henry twirled the brass signet ring on his finger.

The *Maresciallo's* smile was like a threat of violence. "Let us think of it this way. You and Mr. Sims are like two suitors, serenading the loveliest of all things but one, a great fortune."

Henry looked up angrily. "I *really* think . . ."

"Now if the owner of that fortune—let us call him the father of the future bride—discovers that one of his daughter's lovers is a murderer—" he stabbed a finger at Voltor—"the other lover wins. Isn't that correct, sir!"

Henry stood up. His face was red. "I'm afraid I must leave." He moved forward but his way was blocked by a wall of solid official flesh.

"Therefore—the rules of logic constrain me to disregard your alarming story. In the same way I should have to disregard the story of someone who claimed to know nothing about the matter and who would benefit by knowing nothing. Do you follow?"

"I beg your pardon—I must—" Henry was beginning to look liverish.

"So, unless I have positive information to the contrary, I shall report Mrs. Sheridan's death as accidental. Do you have any such information?"

"I've told you already. Please . . ."

"I said *positive*."

"I'm not feeling well. Perhaps another . . ."

Rizzi stared at him unwaveringly for a few seconds. Then he stepped aside. "Yes, you may go. If I need you again I will find you."

Voltor hurried to the door. The *Maresciallo* went to the desk, opened a box and took out a cigar. He examined it, smelled it, and took another. His hand hovered for a third but became conscious of rank and closed the box. So far nothing, except two accusations which not even the most eager novice would credit. "Scavengers"—that adequately described them all. On the other side, his superiors had made it clear that they wanted a report of accidental death. A man might go against higher powers for a reason—but with none at all . . . He shrugged and lit a cigar. In any case he would talk to the secretary; and perhaps to the old man, if he were well enough. He drew deeply on the Havana. Ah, what a splendid way to die!

CHAPTER THIRTEEN

Directly after lunch on the following day, Celia went to the garden. She had found the small door which led to the bridge that morning and had promised herself to go there as soon as she could be alone. Since Saturday it had been an ordeal to be with anyone, especially at mealtimes. She feared her companions at the table more than the police. The three men seldom discussed Mrs. Sheridan's death openly, but their eyes followed her slightest movements, waiting for her to betray herself. Once, William had said, "Of course, the police know it was an accident?" And she had replied, "Of course," without a tremor. She knew he *wanted* them to believe it. *Maresciallo* Rizzi had come for a final interview this morning. He would enter a report of accidental death—because she had lied.

The bridge was very narrow and weeds grew in the cracks of its stone pavement. Two green lizards were sunning themselves on the marble railing. Celia tried to crouch down as she climbed the shallow steps to the top of the arch. But there was something glaringly theatrical about the open canal and the surrounding buildings. One couldn't hide on a stage set. It constantly surprised her that Venice could be made of such solid materials and look so much like a cloth backdrop. She stood straight and walked down the far side of the arch, holding carefully to the railing. The garden would be different.

Just at the end of the bridge an ornate iron gate stood ajar. Through it she could see a gentle lawn, from which occasional tulips and poppies grew as though by accident. Her body relaxed. It was right that she had come, and that it was Sunday. This was a day for visiting the dead, for buying potted plants in a hothouse, for plucking the tiny wings of weeds from dirt mounds. She had once thought that dead bodies themselves made the mounds, that they lay no deeper than an iris stem.

Sundays and death. You might die any time, but you were not truly gone until your memory was overlaid with the drowsy colors of a church window. There you found the deep blue of holy figures, the purple of shadows, the red of Scribes and Pharisees, and green . . . always green in the background. Fern green, wreath green, the color of the cloth in the bottom of the collection plate. In the afternoon the grass of the cemetery lawn stained the soles of your shoes and put mysterious marks on your white dress. A crushed elm leaf lay on the gravel walk and withering dandelion plants, which had been rooted from the swollen earth with her grandmother's shoehorn, lay on either side of the headstones.

Celia dropped to the ground. A few feet from her hand was a yellow tulip. She reached out and touched it. One of her nails bit into the green flesh. How easy it was to break! That, too, would be a murder, but one never thought of it that way. She drew her hand away. It was nice to be again among things that were what they seemed. It brought the truth back. Mrs. Sheridan was dead, but that made no difference now. She would not mind that she had been killed, for there was no way for her to care.

Once more she examined the flowers around her. She

preferred the poppies. But how strange to have them growing directly out of the grass, as though they were figures on a carpet sprung into the third dimension. Then she began to see that she had been wrong about the garden. It was *not* what it seemed. Even here the familiar pattern was repeated. The lawn was closed in by box shrubs, some of which were vaguely shaped to resemble furniture. Except for the sky above she might have been sitting in a small reception room. Again, the novelty was carried too far to be a joke. There was something serious behind it—a fear of things as they were.

Celia stood. At the far end of the "reception room" was an arched doorway. As she approached it, avoiding the flowers, she saw water sparkling and heard the clamor of fountains. There was another room beyond. Someone had carved a house out of a garden.

She was in a great salon, again surrounded by box hedges rising ten or twelve feet. At either end of the room were two splendid stone fountains made from a rough rock that looked like sandstone, but which must have been many times stronger, for it was worked as delicately as cast iron. The fountains were about eight feet tall and plumes of water doubled their height. The spray fell to a floor made of colored tiles and ran back to mossy gutters at the base of each. She walked forward.

Here and there the tiles were interrupted by patches of purple verbena growing in black earth. She stopped. The walls of the room were covered with wisteria vines, bearing blossoms like enormous bunches of grapes. The air was stained lavender. To the left was a large, arched doorway surmounted by a circular silver cage filled with screeching birds. On either side of the cage, a little lower than the top of the arch, were two stationary metal figures, set with plates of colored glass which revolved at the touch of a breeze. Placed irregularly along the walls of the room were solid chunks of purple, green, and rust-colored marble, polished at the tops to serve as benches.

Celia was shocked. She had never seen a garden like this. It was almost obscene to play such tricks on Nature —to dress her up and treat her as though she belonged in a drawing room. Worse than that, to make her seem—unhealthy. A hussy whose only concern was pleasure (not amusement. *That* was all right, but pleasure was a little too amusing). In fact, as she thought of it she grew absolutely prudish. A garden should be Victorian, with demure flowers; trees and shrubs ought to be smug and a little sad. Seeing Nature like *this* was like seeing her own grandmother in a bikini. The spray of the nearest fountain had formed a rainbow. As she walked past, it misted her hair. The air smelled of wet, too-rich earth; and above the ring of falling water she heard swarms of bees at the wisteria. Celia turned toward a spot of brilliant color just visible through the arched doorway.

She noticed that the walls were not only covered with wisteria, but with vines of bougainvillea, so that in warmer weather the room would change from lavender to violet. Beneath the arch she glanced nervously at the chattering birds. She hated to see things in cages *out*-doors. The tile stopped abruptly. Celia stepped past the box hedge wall into a perfectly square enclosure, carpeted with green-and-white ivy. Through it narrow walks of Carrara marble led like spokes of a wheel to a sunken cup of flowers in the center. As she walked forward she noticed that steps descended through the flowers to a stone disk; and on this a large sundial was mounted. But it would have been impossible to tell the time of day except by walking down to it, for the cup blazed with color as though it were full of lighted brandy.

She had never seen such a concentration of colors before in her life. It was almost ugly. Acid yellows were poured into purple, and orange smouldered on lizard-green. The plants were raised or lowered, according to their natural height, so that the blossoms were all on a level. The idea was to throw every hue of a garden into a single receptacle, just to see the fight. It was as though someone were trying to humiliate Nature. Someone—was playing God.

At the far end of the square she found another doorway and this, at last, led into a conventional section of the garden. She recognized the mimosa tree which stood beneath her window. There were several rose bushes in uncontrolled bloom and some small fig trees. In one corner, beside a tool house, were a pile of black earth and fifty or sixty neatly stacked pots. Some stained garden furniture stood beneath the mimosa tree. Celia was relieved. It was like being asked into the kitchen. She took one of the chairs and drew it apart from the others. As she sat down she scuffed her shoes happily in the rough turf.

"I've always thought it was an improvement on Francis Bacon. He used too much space."

Celia turned. Standing beside the tool house was a man in a robe and slippers. A fireman-red handkerchief fluttered from his breast pocket and a cigar was stuck jauntily in his mouth. He appeared a young sixty.

"You don't know how welcome you are, honey."

"Who are you?" she said, pretending—even to herself—that she did not know.

CHAPTER FOURTEEN

William had borrowed the master key from the butler. As the Sunday evening meal was always a simple one, the servants who, except for Massimo and the cook, lived out with their families, normally did not come until early evening to serve and turn down the beds. Today, even Massimo had gone to a christening—and the house was empty of all but its guests. The young man went first to the floor at water level. In a notebook he made a careful list of the contents of the large reception room. Then he visited the two dressing rooms beyond the hall and did the same. At the back of the house were an ample kitchen and pantry. There were also three empty rooms off the corridor, one quite large. This last contained two spiral columns, heavily gilded, supporting nothing. Another held three tapestry-covered chairs. Otherwise all three rooms were unfurnished. The windows, except for those in the kitchen, were barred and tightly shuttered. William closed his notebook and went to the first floor.

Here, he repeated the procedure. At the front of the house, facing the canal, was the study. He carefully listed the contents of this room and then went to the two *sale di rappresentanza* which adjoined. These were "living-rooms," designed for stiff introductions or for the formal calls of ladies who have been nodding to each other at the theater for forty years. There was no apparent reason for there being two. One was furnished in dull pink, the other in dull blue. William noted the contents.

To the right of the *sale di rappresentanza* was an enormous dining room. It was furnished with the elephantine taste of wealthy families who buy for their children's children. For generations, small faces had risen like pretty moons over one edge of the table while old ones withered and dropped past the other edge. The young man looked up from his notebook, frowning. He went to the *credenza* and examined the china's pedigree. He shrugged contemptuously and resumed writing.

Next to the dining room was a large serving pantry, connected with the kitchen by the dumb-waiter. Beyond that were several unused rooms, again unfurnished.

On the second floor—third, by American reckoning—William knocked at Celia's room. He waited a moment, then entered and looked quickly around. He went to the door which connected her room to Mrs. Sheridan's and, standing between both, quickly made a list of their contents.

When he left there was no one in the hall. He paused at both Voltor's and Sims' doors, then hurried down the corridor to the rear of the house. Using Massimo's key he entered a large room adjoined by a bath with a pool-sized bathing tub of black and lemon marble. Beyond that was a dressing room, a salon, and a long gallery with a Bolognese Renaissance table in the center and walls draped in green silk. At regular intervals squares of the material showed a deeper color as though they had been protected by paintings for many years. Except for the massive table in this room, which could not have been easily moved, the apartment was unfurnished. Its windows were tightly shut and it smelled of stale cigar smoke.

The third floor was the same. Aside from Mr. Fox's two rooms, which William did not enter, his own small one and a furnished bedroom to the rear, the rest of the floor was totally bare. The servants' quarters were in the attic. William found one brass bed, an old wardrobe and a cane-bottomed chair in Massimo's room. He didn't bother to look at the cook's. He closed the notebook, put it in his pocket and left the attic.

William stopped at Mr. Fox's door and knocked. He was grinning. Under his breath he recited: ". . . there is a devil haunts thee in the likeness of an old fat man . . ."

He knocked again. ". . . why dost thou converse with that trunk of humours, that bolting-hutch of beastliness, that swollen parcel of dropsies . . ."

Then he leaned his head toward the door panel. His hand dropped to the knob. ". . . that huge bombard of sack, that stuffed cloak-bag of guts, that reverend vice . . ." The door was locked. He was reaching to his pocket for the master key when he heard a step in the corridor behind him. His shoulders suddenly relaxed and he pulled at the knob as though gently closing the door. William turned, smiling faintly to himself, as a man might who has tiptoed successfully from a bedside.

"Good afternoon, sir. May I help you?" He blocked the way.

"No thank you. I wish to see Mr. Fox."

"I'm afraid not now, Mr. Voltor. He is very weak today."

"Please let me by."

William sighed. "Very well. He was hoping to get

some rest before the lawyer came. But I'm sure . . ."

"Lawyer! Great heavens. It's decided?"

The young man looked astonished. "You mean you didn't know? I thought surely *you* would."

"You mean, I . . ." Henry's face was trembling at the edge of confidence.

William nodded, solemnly. "You expected it?"

The weak blue eyes seemed about to flood with tears. "I had some reason to think it—yes." The mouth began to relax.

"Mr. Fox is very fond of you, sir."

Henry mumbled something.

"What did you say?"

"Nothing. Marrakech, I was thinking of Marrakech."

"I can't understand why he's waited so long. The choice seemed obvious from the start. He really can't last more than a few days . . ." William looked nervously at the door and drew Henry Voltor away. "He may not be *quite* asleep." He pushed the older man down the hall.

"You don't think I should look in for a moment? Poor chap."

"No—he would be displeased. Not with you, of course. With me." They stopped at the elevator and the young man opened the doors. He smiled conspiratorially at Voltor. "Am I wrong in assuming you have done Mr. Fox a service, sir? Recently?"

Henry stepped into the car. His voice was light. "Yes, I was able to help him with something."

"Ah, that explains it."

"Explains what?"

"His asking for the lawyer today. He'd already waited so long that I thought today, being Sunday . . ."

Henry's eyes sparkled. "He insisted?"

William nodded. "Gratitude." He pushed the button marked "1" and they started down.

"I confess, I expected something like this."

"It was an excellent move, sir."

"Yes, it appears. In the beginning I was not quite easy, but . . ."

"You lent him money?"

There was no reply.

The car stopped and William opened the doors. "Would you like a drink, Mr. Voltor? It's a little early in the day, but perhaps this is an exceptional day."

"Yes, I think I might have a spot."

"You said you lent him money? How fortunate he was to have someone to turn to." They went toward the library, William slightly to the rear.

"Poor chap's been bed-ridden so long he hasn't been able to . . ." Henry glanced back at the young man. "Of course you know that."

"He always insisted on handling his financial affairs personally." They reached the library door. William held it open and waited for Voltor to precede him. "A great deal of money?" He went to the table and found some ice in the thermodor.

"Rather." Henry's voice grew almost coy.

"Martini?"

"Yes. That will go splendidly."

"A few hundred—or more?"

Henry attempted the enigmatic smile of a Greek gambler. "Five thousand."

"Pounds!" Vermouth jumped into the mixing glass.

"There were a number of pressing commitments apparently." He paused. "You know that also, I'm sure."

William flooded the drinks with gin. "Of course. I doubt that he'll do much with the money. He likes the idea of settling his accounts before he dies, but there isn't much time. I don't think he knows how near the end he is."

Henry smiled. "I understand perfectly. Men of his stamp wish to be square with the world when they leave it."

William handed him a martini, filled to the brim. "You're quite right. I'm sure you have no cause to worry."

"Worry?"

"None. After all, five thousand pounds is a considerable amount. I expect you don't have an IOU?"

Voltor's face grew sallow. "What?"

"That is, of course, if you *aren't* the beneficiary. If you are that's a different matter."

The drink splashed down his sleeve. "If I'm *not* the beneficiary?"

"Sorry, use my handkerchief. Yes, if you're not. I'm certain he'll remember to pay you back, somehow."

"But you said I *was!*"

William looked puzzled. "I said what? I thought *you* knew, sir. You told me . . ."

Voltor's voice hardened. "I told you nothing. You said—or implied—that I had been named in Mr. Fox's will."

"I may have. I took it for granted because you seemed so sure. Of course you might be named. You might, you know." William drained his glass.

"It is quite clear that you believe I will not be, and that you have deliberately made me think otherwise. It is also quite clear that I have advanced five thousand pounds to Mr. Fox on the assumption that I should be made chief beneficiary of his will. I demand now that you tell me your reason for believing I will not be." For a moment Henry's expression achieved the nobility of his blood. He bore that look of dedicated greed, firm in adversity, which for hundreds of years had distinguished his ancestors from ordinary men.

William shook his head. "I haven't any *real* reason."

"What is it! You must tell me!"

"Well, it's Mr. Sims." The young man refilled their glasses. "Perhaps I shouldn't say this . . ."

"Say it!"

"Mr. Sims appears to think that I can influence Mr. Fox's choice—somewhat."

Henry's sigh was like a wind keening in cypress.

"He has offered me a quarter of his inheritance for my services." William smiled wryly. "I've already told him not to count on me absolutely, but he seems to think . . ."

"How much do you want to work for me, instead." The voice had a desperate courage.

William lowered his eyes. "Really, sir. I'm afraid I would be of very little use to you. The old man trusts me, of course, but . . ."

"How much?"

"Half."

"No!"

William walked over to the book shelves. He took out a book, flipped the pages and smiled. "Yes."

"What's to keep me from reporting you to your employer?"

"The fear that I'll report you. I have only a job to lose. You have a fortune. Or half a fortune."

Henry looked momentarily hopeful. "Even if I did promise, you couldn't hold me to it."

William closed his book on one finger. "You give me an IOU for half of everything you possess over your present worth, collectible any time. Don't worry, I *know* your present worth. It isn't much."

"And if I do this I will be named sole heir?"

"That depends." William opened the book to the place he had marked. "Listen:

> '*When you do come to swim in golden lard,*
> *Up to the arms in honey that your chin*
> *Is borne up stiff with fatness of the flood*
> ....*remember me.*' "

"What nonsense is this?"

"Very familiar nonsense, sir." He replaced the book. "You can give me the IOU any time this evening."

Voltor sighed. It was defeat.

"But that isn't all."

"Oh my God!"

"Whether you inherit or not I shall have to have a retainer."

Henry closed his eyes. "Retainer?"

"Of course."

"How much?"

"Five thousand pounds. You can give me a check for that tonight, also."

The old man's glass trembled. "But this is outrageous!"

William approached him gravely. "It certainly is." He took Henry by the arm and led him to the chair in the center of the room. "The one disadvantage in trying to be excessively rich," he said, "is that there is so damn much competition."

CHAPTER FIFTEEN

"You're Miss Johns?"

She nodded, and slowly got up from her garden chair.

He pulled the red handkerchief from the pocket of his robe and wiped his perspiring head. "Do you think you can answer a question?" His slippers were made of flaming, tooled leather.

"Yes . . ." she said, timidly.

"Any question?"

"Well, it does depend on the question, a little."

"Of course it does. Why do you wear stockings which make your legs look as though they were bare?"

"Is that the question?"

"Uh-huh."

"How do you know they aren't bare?"

He adjusted his silk belt over an ample but well-proportioned stomach. "Thank you. Of course I *do* know they aren't. I don't know why. That's what you mean?"

"Yes." She resisted the temptation to look down at her legs. They felt warm with admiration. "And now may I ask you a question? Rather, repeat one?"

"You may."

"Who are you?"

"My name is Fox." He chuckled. "I'm sick in bed up

there." He pointed to the top story of his house, just visible over the garden wall.

"Then you're *not* sick?"

He frowned. "Sometimes I feel better than other times."

"And you feel better now?"

"A little." He looked at her thoughtfully. "Thanks to you."

"How—thanks to me?"

"Youth is contagious."

"But if you're not *really* ill, that means . . ."

"Abstractly, nothing at all. It means something to the people concerned. You are not."

"No, but . . ."

"You aren't, are you?"

"No, I'm not."

"Very well. There are always present things to occupy us. What do you think of my garden?"

She resumed her seat. "I like this part of it much better."

He looked shocked. "Lord help me, kitten, you got sharper eyes than that."

She shrugged. "I do though."

"I do though," he mocked. "Why are the poor so smug about having nothing?"

She sat up straight. "I'm not rich, Mr. Fox. I work for my living—or I did. But I don't see that this gives you the right . . ."

"Damnit. That's enough!" The old man's face was flushed. He stood in front of her, the legs of his pajamas spread wide. "Remember you're my guest."

"I am fully aware of that, sir. I will not impose on you any longer. I . . ."

"Oh cut it out. All this cheap-jack talk turns my stomach. I don't care if you're poor, but don't *want* to be."

"As a matter of fact I don't . . ." Her eyes were bright. She knew they looked well. ". . . anyway, I don't see what that has to do with my liking this part of your garden better."

Mr. Fox drew up a chair next to her. "Because, honey —a thing that's poor is poor. And rich, believe it or not, is rich. A long time ago everybody knew that—like they knew how to add. But lately the simplest ideas in the world are stood on their heads. You can train a man to choose a rag rug over a Heris, painted plywood over walnut, and even a cigarette over a cigar. He can be taught to take less for more and kiss your foot for it. He likes his foods 'simple,' his thoughts 'comfortable,' his laxatives 'natural.' He's a mess. You don't want to be a mess, dolly. I worked on that garden. It cost time and patience and money. Mostly money. It's rich. It may make your belly ache but it's worth it. I left this part alone just to show what a sloppy job you can expect from Nature. Now *don't* go telling me you like it better. Hear?"

Celia was silent for a moment. Then she pursed her lips. "But I do like it better."

Curiously, his anger vanished. "I think you'll do," he said.

"What are you talking about?"

"I mean you can stay here as long as you like. Free." He leaned forward and placed a hand on her knee, not quite impersonally. "You're welcome to the works, honey. We'll get this bunch cleaned out of here tomorrow and . . ."

She jumped up. Her face was pale. "No—please!"

His large blue eyes were reproachful. "You can at least wait until . . ."

"I . . . think I'd better go." She began to draw away.

He made an impatient gesture. "This's what happens when women are raised by women. Don't tell me you weren't!"

He seemed to be accusing *her*. She nodded, slowly.

He stood up and walked sorrowfully to the mimosa tree. His voice was thick with forced forgiveness. "It's not all your fault, honey. There ought to be a law!" He broke a yellow plume from the tree and returned with it. "Here, wear that somewhere. You got good color for it."

She took it. Celia knew she was blushing. "Excuse me, I thought you meant . . ."

"That I was propositioning you?"

"Yes."

"I am."

"Well, I . . ." Her indignation rushed back, without the fear this time.

Mr. Fox raised an agreeably furry hand. "Speak of it no more. For the time being the invitation's open anyway. We can discuss your problems after the others are gone. You'd better wear it at the collar of your dress. Never keep cut mimosa around for more than three hours. The smell curdles."

Celia obediently drew a pin from under her collar. "You were a friend of Mrs. Sheridan's," she said, at last. She was afraid she had put too much emphasis on the word "friend."

"Of course not—I lived with her once, that's all." He looked at her through squinted eyes. "You won't believe it, but her complexion was better than yours."

Celia thought of the old lady's loose back and the painful wrinkles under her eyes . . . eyes which had now dried and cracked. "But she was your friend. She came to you when she thought . . ."

Mr. Fox bared his perfect teeth. "You know better than that."

She nodded, slowly. "Yes, I do. But if you aren't really sick I don't know what to think."

He came near and took her hand. Celia wanted to draw away but she was afraid of insulting him. She tried to smile. One of his hands was already at her elbow. "Is it important for you to know what to think?"

She nodded. "Yes, it is. I—I wonder if I could sit down?" He led her solicitously to a chair and sat opposite her, refusing to release the hand.

"Well, then it's simple. I was having a joke. I'm sure you think it was not quite a nice joke, but I'm older than you are and I've got to work for my amusement. Then the old beast died."

And now the "old beast" was lying still and alone—where?

"After that I lost interest in the game."

"Do you mean to say you've brought these people here deliberately to make fools of them? I—I think that's sadistic."

Cecil dropped the girl's hand. "God, I wish I had a drink. Listen, young lady. A thing is sadistic not when you think it is but when the Marquis de Sade thinks it is. He'd have thought this was a Sunday school romp. Just good fun. Now let's forget it and talk about how you're going to have your hair cut. Some things have got to be taken care of if you stay around here."

"Does that mean William—Mr. Fieramosca also knew about the joke?"

He looked at her, sharply. "Sure. Why shouldn't he?"

"No reason."

"He's an actor, dolly. Didn't he tell you that? They're freaks. I'll get rid of him, too. We'll be all alone."

"But there has to be some reason . . ." She stopped and stared down at her hands. . . . Some reason for the murder. She *knew* it was murder, but if it was true that William had known all the time it was a joke . . .

"Reason for what? I'm afraid you talk to yourself, girl. That's only a good habit when you're alone—like picking your nose."

She looked up, confused. "Nothing. I was just thinking."

"Did she leave you broke? You don't have to tell me. She did her best to leave everyone that way."

"I have a little," Celia said, trying to make the "little" sound restrained rather than exaggerated.

"I hope you clipped her. If I'd known I could have hid her stuff for you until the police had gone. What'd they say to you?" Mr. Fox leaned back in his chair. The two iron legs sank into the turf. The long ash of his cigar dropped to his silken paunch. His motions were elaborately casual.

"He just asked a lot of questions . . . There was only one. His name was Rizzi."

"Yes, I talked to him yesterday. Do you know how he reported the death?"

"He reported an accident," she said, slowly.

There was a pause. "And do you think it was?"

She spread her hands. "What else could it be? I don't think she committed suicide."

He tossed the cigar butt to the ground, where it lay,

smouldering. "No. There are only two ways to commit suicide. One is to be so mentally under age you can't believe you will die, and the other is to be so ripe you can't believe anything else. Old Crow was in between. So she must have got one pill too many and gone off her nut."

"Old Crow?"

"That's what I called her, on account of the birthmark on her . . . Good Lord, girl! A man can't say five successive words to you without your tensing up like a garden party hostess with a bumblebee in her brassiere. You're making me nervous. Come off it."

Deep in her memory Celia caught a familiar echo. Something about a crow or a raven. . . . Then it was gone. "I'm sorry." To change the subject, she said, "Have you been here long?"

"Nope—I came just a minute ago." He nodded toward the tool shed. "There's a door there, to the street."

"The street!"

"That's right."

"But you're not dressed for the street. She stared at the screaming pajama legs and slippers. "You can't walk through the street like that."

"You mean they'll arrest me? I assure you they won't."

"No—I didn't mean that. It's just . . . other people."

"What about other people?"

"Well, they might object. After all, you *aren't* wearing very conventional clothes."

"That's exactly why they wouldn't dare say anything, honey—that and the fact that I'm rich. Every man out there is convinced that everyone else is just a little bit better than he is. Not one of them has enough conceit to stuff a raisin. They may pretend they have, but they don't *really*. That's a thing you have to remember. People hate themselves because they think they're not as good as you are. They may get around to hating you but it takes a while. In the meantime you can keep them doing what you damn please."

"But what's that got to do with walking through the street in your pajamas? Why didn't you come across your own bridge, for heaven's sake?"

"It hasn't got anything to do with it. I'm just telling you who runs things around here. I didn't come across my bridge because there're still people in my house who think I'm dying upstairs. We'll clear them out tomorrow. Then you and I can have a little time for ourselves."

"First of all," Celia said, primly, "I'm not staying. Second, I just wonder how you're going to get your guests to leave?"

Mr. Fox grinned. "Don't worry. They're going out tomorrow."

"You can't throw them out."

"I could, but I won't. I don't have to. Why are you going, dolly? Don't you like my place?"

"Because there're some things you can't buy, Mr. Fox—and some people."

He smiled, sadly. "You're not using your head. If I were going to buy you I wouldn't tip you off ahead of time. Your price would go up. I'm no damn fool."

She was silent for a long time. Then she bowed her head. "I suppose I'm the one who's a fool. I haven't even got fare home. And after all, the one thing worse than being bought is having no one make an offer, isn't it?"

He frowned. "How old are you?"

"Twenty."

"Parents?"

"They're dead."

"Say that again."

"I said my parents were dead."

He stood up and came to her side. Taking her chin in his hand he made her look up at him. "I'd swear you were one of us."

She pulled her head away.

"It's in the mouth. Not so much the eyes, the mouth." He touched her cheek with the tips of his fingers.

"What are you talking about?" Her voice had taken on an edge.

"The Cocks and Lions."

She stood up also, not liking to feel herself cornered. "Now *you're* talking to yourself."

"No—I just said you were a member of the Cocks and Lions. Not a very firm one, but you're a member all the same. You can march in our annual parades—if we ever have any parades, which we won't."

"I don't know what you're talking about."

"It's probably just as well you haven't learned sooner."

"Please." She turned toward him, sharply. "I don't like whimsy."

He looked at her, solemnly. "This isn't. I have just made you acquainted with one of the most important facts of your life. It will explain a great many things about you which always wanted explaining."

She was struck by his sobriety. "Then—I don't understand. What is the Cocks and Lions?"

"It's a club without a headquarters, without officers

and without a function. It probably has something between a million and two million members all over the world, among which are some of the most depraved and most innocent examples of the human race." He took her arm and led her toward the center gardens. This time the hand did not explore.

She stepped through the hedge, into the garden of ivy and flowers. "And I am . . ."

"One of the innocents, dolly. But that's just a word they use outside. In the club it doesn't mean anything. We're incorruptible so it doesn't make any difference how corrupt we are. Hell's bells, girl—you know what I mean."

"Perhaps . . ." Celia said.

"As I told you, you'll never advance much. Even I haven't. I mean a thirty-second degree Cocks and Lions is screaming out his lungs in a mad house. That's the kind of club it is. Most of our best people never get past the age of twenty."

"You mean we're . . . they're sick?"

"Not at all, kitten. We're well. That's just the trouble. The whole damn world's a hospital, run by the patients. If you got nothing wrong with you they throw you in a bed and force-feed you bland food until you're as weak as they are. That is, they'll do it if you let 'em."

"I don't know who you mean by 'they.' "

"Don't be silly. Everyone who isn't us."

"I'm not so sure who we are."

"Everyone who isn't them." He led her along a path of Carrara to the edge of the bowl of flowers. "What more do you want, honey. I just made you a member of the club."

"But I still don't understand what the club is."

"My dear, it's a league of depraved saints and pristine scoundrels." He took her hand and with a courtly gesture began to lead her down to the sundial. It looked like a large, obscene flower. "For the rest you'll have to look at yourself."

"Do you know what I think?" she said, following obediently.

"What?"

"That you made all this up a moment ago."

"In fact I didn't, honey. Though if I had, it wouldn't have been any the less true. Forty years ago a woman told me about the Cocks and Lions." He stopped at the center and turned to her. "She explained it just as I am explaining it to you, with a few modifications, perhaps."

"What modifications?"

"Never mind, honey. The younger generation's too thin-skinned. The whole lousy race is dying out if you ask me. Anyway, since then I've met three other members. You're the fourth."

"I'm not sure I want to be the fourth."

"Nothing to be ashamed of, dolly. As I said, we're incorruptible, so why not be? But it's not necessary, really. You can *act* as virtuous as you please."

The sundial, Celia noticed, was of ordinary white plaster. Around the top it was marred by pock marks at regular intervals. However, in the place of XII on the dial, was a large blue stone. The sunlight blazed in its heart.

"All right," she said. "You didn't make it up. But you have no proof that I'm one of these people. What makes you so sure?"

Mr. Fox reached down, groaning, and picked up a potsherd. "You have the first qualification, honey. All the others follow." He began to scratch away the plaster around the stone.

"What is that?"

"You know. Why should I tell you?"

"I'd like to hear."

He blew away some of the plaster. The blue stone glistened.

"What do you know best in the world?"

"Best? Why—nothing."

"I don't mean what you learned in school. Just tell me the thing you know best."

"No, really . . ."

He straightened up. "The reason you won't is because you can't imagine I know."

"I don't understand what you're talking about."

"Yes you do. What do you know best in the world?"

"Nothing. I swear."

He smiled and resumed digging around the blue stone. "There is something you know better than most people, isn't there?"

"No, really. I . . ."

"You see."

"But that's not . . ."

"Yes it is. That's *just* what I meant." He placed his thumb on the stone and pushed.

"I know . . ."

"Go on."

"I know how people die."

The stone came loose from the plaster. Mr. Fox took it in his hand and held it in the sunlight. "Exactly."

"But surely there's not a *club* of people who know such things. Besides—everybody does, a little."

"You're wrong. *No*body does. They pretend they do, just as they pretend most other things. But when you really know there's a difference. It shows in your face and in the way you speak of dying. Once you know how people die you never live the same again. You understand, it isn't the dying itself that's important. It's *how*—as you said." He polished the blue stone on the lapel of his robe and tossed it in the air.

"I—I don't think I'd like to speak of it any more. Maybe you're right, but I . . ."

"Of course. Here, take this. It's yours." He thrust the stone in her hand.

"What is it?"

"A sapphire. A good one, too. If you don't have to sell it soon, keep it for luck."

She stared at it. "It's not real?"

"Of course it is. As you see, there used to be others. I gave the rest away with a good deal more provocation."

"I'm sorry, but I can't take it."

"Why?" He was going to be angry again.

"Because you obviously mean this as a . . . I just won't accept presents from you, that's all."

"But I'm asking you to take it," he said, stepping close.

"I am very sorry but—ouch!"

"Will you take it now?"

"You can't do that—please!"

"Take it."

"You're out of your mind. I never led you to assume . . . Oh!" She backed away from him, holding the stone in her clenched fist. Her face was geranium red.

Mr. Fox followed. "Not another word about the sapphire, see? And no more pious remarks about what you've never led me to assume—or I will."

"Please—I don't want this. You must take it back. I'm sure you don't understand . . ."

He began to follow her up the stairs. "Are you going to take it or not?"

She backed up, between the tiers of flowers. She was afraid to turn around and run.

"Well?" He had nearly reached her.

"Yes," she said, breathlessly. Then she added a low, "Thank you."

Five minutes later, when they were walking in the garden with the fountains, Celia stopped and turned to her friend. "What has Francis Bacon got to do with it?"

"With what?"

"This. You mentioned him when you first spoke to me. You said it was an improvement. I thought you meant the garden."

"I did. Francis once decided he was going to tell everyone how to build a garden—everyone with more than a few million, of course. I took some things from him."

"You mean ideas?"

"With a couple of million, ideas *are* things, honey." He pointed to the bird cage. "The birds, for instance. That's a good touch. Caged. And those decorations on either side are his. Caged lights. Same thing."

"But didn't you say he used too much space?"

"Yes. No shape. Or none you could see except if you were in an airplane. I kept his idea for carpentry work on shrubbery—you can get good shapes that way—but I cut out the heath and his God damn endless promenades. Elizabethan England was a little like Hollywood. The old fraud even had a swimming pool. Anyway this is Venice and there're not more than forty acres of land in the whole city—or I might have tried it . . . What's the matter?"

Celia tried to smile. "Nothing. I was just thinking."

"Good God, again. What is it?"

She looked down at a bed of verbena. Finally she said, "Just thinking."

"Don't pull a ligament."

She tried to stop her mind. "What lovely little flowers," she said. But her thoughts raced on. She knew now why William had murdered Mrs. Sheridan—and whom he would murder next.

CHAPTER SIXTEEN

"Where were you?" William said, locking the door behind him. "I came up here twice and you weren't in."

"Then I must have been out." Fox was in bed with a bottle of Old Dan'l and the Space Falcon.

"You're crazy. Did anyone see you?"

"Impossible. I had my vision-field reverser turned on. No one could have seen me without Meloride space warpers."

"Why do you take the trouble to convince everyone you're dying if you're going to give the show away at the last act?"

Cecil threw down his book. He had changed to a white dressing gown with lime green piping. His pajamas were navy blue with gold scarabs. "I'm sick of it. There's no kick left in this damn business."

"You've lost a wife. That should make up for it."

"I'd just as soon have lost her a couple of days later." Cecil sat on the edge of the bed and put his bottle on the floor. He shuffled his feet into a pair of milk-white slippers. "You get a thing planned right down to the nub and *every* time something happens," he said, morosely.

"You can still go through with it."

The old man shrugged. "It's like putting on Hamlet without Ophelia."

"That could be done, too."

"Lord, boy, I'm in this for kicks. If it isn't fun I

don't want to do it." He looked up at William, sharply.

His secretary grinned. "If *I* took five thousand pounds in one haul I wouldn't worry about the fun."

"He told you?" Cecil affected modesty.

"I urged him. Did you get the same from Sims?"

"He wanted to do a little something for me."

William approached the bed and picked up the bottle. "You smell like a still."

The old man yawned. "Take my advice, boy. Get yourself a couple of solid dissipations and stick to them."

"Why did you go out?"

". . . that way you don't go ruining your health. Look at sleeping pills, for instance—or that God damned cocaine."

"You've swindled two of your guests and the only reason you're sorry the third one died is because you missed the chance to swindle her."

". . . Now marijuana—that's silly. What's worse, it's not dignified. Alcohol and nicotine are the best of the lot . . ."

"So why go out and risk everything at the last minute?" He cleared the night-table on the near side of the bed and put the bottle on it.

". . . outside of high-grade opium maybe. Listen, boy, I didn't hire a keeper."

William went to the desk and took out the deck of cards. "I'm not trying to be one. But you did hire me to do a job. I thought it was just a joke at first but that doesn't matter now. I want to see the production come off." He tossed the cards down on the bed and drew up a chair.

"Look—if you think I arranged all this for the chicken-feed I got from those two *affamati* you're dippy.

Even if it were a lot more I wouldn't have. I do things for the hell of it first and for cash second. What's the ante?"

"Same as usual." William emptied the coins from his pocket. "You still haven't answered my question."

Mr. Fox took the bottle from the table. "I'll think about it. The *carabinieri* have dropped the case, haven't they?"

"Yes. Rizzi was here this morning again. What did you think of him yesterday?"

"Smart. Get the cigars. You know where they are."

The young man stood up and went around the bed. "He's sending in his report."

"Accidental death?"

"Yes. The girl helped."

The bottle left Cecil's lips with a long kiss. "Then you *don't* think it was?"

William returned with a handful of cigars which he passed to his employer, keeping two for himself. "Of course I do. I mean thanks to the girl he filed the report so quickly. Rizzi didn't bother you today, did he?"

"No." Cecil spit out the tip of his cigar.

"I told him you were in bad shape."

They lit up. Clouds of fresh smoke filled the room.

"Thoughtful of you."

"I knew you wouldn't want the police around any more than you could help. There're laws against extortion that might embarrass you."

"Nonsense. You don't call ordinary, everyday winnings extortion." Cecil cut the cards.

"Maybe you don't but *they* certainly will. That's why I don't understand your going out. Where did you go, anyway? You couldn't have got far."

"Not far, no. Down to the garden." He handed the pack to William. "By the way, Sims and Voltor are leaving tomorrow. Everything's ready."

"The will's made?" The young man began to deal.

"I had it written the day you came. You know what to do. You're to read it there, in the sitting room, with all the stops out. I want a good performance, from you, at least. It would have been better with Old Crow, but we'll see what you make of it."

"It ought to be built up more, you know that."

"Do what you can."

"All right, but you should let them stew a day more." William gathered up his cards with quick, nervous fingers.

"They leave tomorrow." Cecil chewed his cigar and studied his hand. "By the way—you're leaving too." He threw the cards face down on the bed.

"You afraid I'll blackmail you? I probably could, you know."

The clock on the mantel chimed and Pierrette's lover resumed his amorous attentions.

"You know better. Not one of you has any proof of anything. Our two guests don't even have endorsed checks as receipts. If you tried to grab, boy, you'd get nothing. When you leave peacefully I'll give you a small bonus. That's all."

"And my salary?"

"Certainly."

"Cards?"

"One."

"When do you want them out?"

"In the morning."

"Why the rush?"

"I've got other plans."

William took up a stack of quarters and tossed them on the bed. "Raise you double. What plans?"

"They don't concern you."

"I see. Straight flush."

"Why do I always lose when you deal?" Cecil took another swig from Old Dan'l.

William tipped back in his chair. "Do you know what I think?"

"Not interested. Come on, play."

"I think you left your room today to see somebody. Maybe your two friends have no proof that they gave you money but if they saw you walking around they'd be bound to make trouble."

The old man smiled benignly. "Haven't you heard, boy? The one virtue of superficial friends is that they always forgive you."

"Still, why take that risk today when you have me to get rid of them for you tomorrow?"

"None of your business. Raise the ante?"

"No. Who did you see, the girl?"

"Start off with a decent pot anyway. Give me a chance to make up."

"Nothing doing. You can't keep your hands off money, can you?" William arranged a pile of change on the bed table beside him . . . "or women."

"You have a fair touch yourself."

"Did you see her?" William's voice was hard.

"What would an old gentleman like me do with a sweet thing like her?" Cecil looked at William with innocent blue eyes as he mechanically dealt the cards.

"How do you know she's a sweet thing?"

"All right—I saw her. She was walking in the garden.

That sounds like a song, doesn't it. You know, John McCormick on that kind of phonograph record that breaks—but that's before your time. I thought she'd like someone to show her around."

William collected his cards. A tiny vein throbbed at his left temple. "Was that the only reason?"

"Oh, I wanted to hear what the *carabiniere* had said."

The young man replaced one card in file and sat back. "And then you decided to make a pass at her?"

"I'm afraid you're mistaking your own intentions for mine, young man." Cecil examined his hand and masked his delight with an inept frown.

William stood up. "You may be smart enough at other things, Mr. Fox, but you have no face for poker. And you don't succeed in hiding your other intentions, either."

The great red face dropped. "You won't play it out?"

"No—take the pot." William went across the room for a glass. "What'd she say when she found out you weren't sick?"

"She thinks I'm a sadist. I'll never have another hand like that."

"Weren't you afraid she'd tell the others?" He came back and poured himself a drink.

"Not very. I'll cut you for all the change that's lying out."

William nodded. "All right. One cut." He shuffled the pack. "What did she say about me?"

Cecil chuckled. "Very little." He cut the pack and held up the king of hearts. "She wanted to know if you were in on the fun."

William stood before the old man. He made no move to take a card. "And what did you say?"

"I said yes, of course. I think she's guessed the whole business. Cut, sucker."

"What do you mean? . . . Everything?"

"Yes. We were talking about Elizabethan England—that's what I mean, boy. Where else are you going to find a girl with a figure like that who can talk . . . Are you going to cut or do you want to forfeit?"

Wililam was rigid. "And . . . ?"

"I think she got it. Nothing to be surprised about. Nice girl. I'm going to give the poor thing a home for a while." Cecil flourished his card smugly and reached to the table for William's money.

"Just a minute." The young man leaned down and cut the remainder of the pack. He held up a card without looking at it. "I'm going to call this a win," he said, quietly. "I nicked the card while you were nicking yours. I just cheated a point higher, that's all." He flipped the ace of spades up on the bed and gathered in the change.

CHAPTER SEVENTEEN

Celia found the book in the library. It was even standing out of line from its neighbors. Of course Mr. Fox would not bother to hide it. That would be part of the game. People liked to play fair in order to be able to laugh louder when they won. She had an hour before dinner. The others were upstairs dressing. She hadn't looked at the play since her sophomore year in college, but she remembered it fairly well. She wanted to reread the end.

Half an hour later she laid the book on the arm of her chair. It was dark outside but the shutters were still open to the canal. The table lamp beside her cast long shadows toward either end of the room. She heard the sputter of an outboard motor and a shout from a barge man. Three hundred and fifty years had changed nearly everything in the city—the buildings, the very water in the canals. But the most fragile thing hadn't been touched. The nature of its people.

She caressed the slender green spine of the book with the tips of her fingers. Mr. Fox was wrong. She did not mind his game. It always surprised her that she could act the part of an innocent young girl so faithfully, while at least half of herself sat back and smiled and refused to be shocked by anything. It had been the same with Mrs. Sheridan's death. She had wept spontaneously and easily when they had taken her body away, but all the while, with a part of her mind, she was wondering if she mightn't pretend that the odd piece of the old lady's luggage was her own. Not the contents, just the bag itself. Her own large one was very shabby. She wasn't being heartless. It was just that when Death came it was a simple fact like any other. One didn't feel sorry for the dead, only for those about to die.

That was why she had to do something now. There would be another death soon unless she found a way to stop it. She was not sentimental about it; and, strangely, she did not resent the fact that the murderer had used her almost as an accomplice in Mrs. Sheridan's death. But she would not allow him to destroy a human life when it was in her power to save it. She could never again be indifferent to dying if she grew indifferent to living also.

She felt about William Fieramosca now exactly as she had felt watching that foolish movie. On the one hand she knew he was an evil man. He frightened and even repelled her. On the other, he was her friend. She had so few friends that she could not afford to divide them into categories as other people did—some "good" some "casual." She had to take what was offered and the fact that this friend was perhaps also capable of murdering *her* was something completely apart. There was a person within her, calm and disturbingly cynical about serious matters, who was not frightened at all—nor the least bit repelled. After all, how many times might she have been offered a seat in a bus or given a place in an elevator by men who had committed murder sometime in their lives? For all she knew it had happened often; and was she to feel any the less grateful to them for being nice to her because they were otherwise antisocial? William had given her a pleasant evening. She still appreciated it, though she tried not to. The person inside informed her, coldly, that he had killed Mrs. Sheridan because he had a plan to get money—a great deal of money. He would not harm *her* as long as she was quiet. More than that, she might even gain.

Celia looked around the shadowy room. Was she really willing to become the accomplice to a murder—to two murders—for money? Surely she had more respect for herself than that! Surely . . . But the voice within her continued to speak—unashamed.

Suddenly she snapped up the book and hid it behind her. There was no noise from the hall, but she knew he was near. She stared at the door. It opened.

"I was hoping to find you alone," William said.

"The others are upstairs dressing. They'll be down in a while." His eyes seemed darker. Proudfly. What an incredibly perfect name.

"Were you busy?"

Her hands were suspiciously empty. "No—I was just sitting."

"I see." He hesitated a moment. Then he smiled. "It can't be very pleasant to sit alone, doing nothing."

"I—like it."

William came across the room and stood beside her. She noticed the thickness of his shoulders. His beard was blue on his cheeks. "Have you been here long?"

"I came only a while ago."

He looked toward the bookshelves. "You might be interested in some of these books. The old man has some good things."

"Yes—perhaps later."

"Especially the Elizabethans. Ford, Greene, Marlowe, Jonson . . ."

"Yes—I must read them . . ."

He turned and walked to the bookshelves. "I sometimes think Mr. Fox was born at least three centuries too late. He's like a character in an old play." He ran his hand along the back of the books. "There's really nothing like them in the world, except the Old Testament. Have you ever read *The Duchess of Malfi?* Or *Volpone?*" His hand stopped at the empty space and he turned to her. His voice had fallen at the last word.

Celia stared at him.

He came back to her side. "I think we understand each other."

She held his eyes for a moment, then looked down. "Yes, we do."

"I hope you aren't getting yourself mixed up in this business."

"What do you mean?"

"It shouldn't be necessary to repeat. It's no longer a simple game—much less a safe one." He loomed over her. She felt as though *she* were being accused of a crime.

"Unfortunately, I'm already involved," she said, at last.

He drew up a small gold chair and sat down. "Do you think so?"

Suddenly she lost patience. "Please," she said. "I'm not such an idiot and I'm not afraid of you."

He rubbed the back of his hand slowly along one cheek. "I never thought you were an idiot," he said. "I realize that you have guessed a good deal of what has been going on in this house. I'm only asking you now to stop. For one day you are to forget the whole thing. Then . . ." He leaned forward, searching her eyes.

"Then?"

"Whatever you want."

"That sounds like a bribe."

"I'm asking you to forget all of this until tomorrow afternoon. As a favor."

Celia reached behind her and took out the book. "Here," she said, handing it to him. "I've done you too many favors already."

He took the book and tossed it on the table. "I don't know that you've done any, so far."

She stood up. "Then you should know that I deliberately withheld proof from the police that you killed Mrs Sheridan."

"Proof?" He looked surprised.

"The pills I left on her table were *not* sleeping pills. But the bottle was emptied as though she had taken them. She was killed and the pills were taken to make it seem she had committed suicide or taken them by accident."

William bit his lip. For a moment he studied her face as though she were a stranger. Then he smiled. "That's hardly proof that *I* killed her. I don't know if it proves anyone did. She might still have taken the pills herself."

"And died a natural death two or three hours after she went to bed in perfect health? Besides, she couldn't have taken all those pills by accident if they hadn't contained a drug. And I know they didn't."

He shifted uneasily. "What did they contain?"

"Sugar. I used them for the second dose every night because I didn't want her to get too much."

"She could still have intended to commit suicide . . ."

Celia went to the table and picked up the book. When she turned to him there were tears in her eyes. "What are you trying to do now? I've already lied for you. I didn't tell the police what I knew. I didn't tell *Maresciallo* Rizzi that you weren't with me all the time at the movie. I didn't tell him about the false sleeping pills—nor even the one thing which I *know* connects you to the murder. I protected you because the old woman was dead and nothing I could do would bring her back. I protected you also because I think of you as my friend, no matter what you are. What's more, I'll go on protecting you. You needn't be afraid of me. But this . . ." She held out the green leather book. "If you try to go through with this I'll go straight to the police. I've already acted foolishly, but that's over. I won't let you do what you're planning."

William stood up and came to her side. "*What* other thing?" he said.

She would not move back as he approached. "The coins. You stole them from her. I don't know why. It seems very stupid. It's the one thing I can't understand about this. When *Maresciallo* Rizzi made me look at every thing in Mrs. Sheridan's bag I noticed that they were missing. She carried rolls of United States coins with her. They were all gone. Then I remembered that I had heard you pay the gondolier in *silver* on Friday night after we came from the movie. I knew you couldn't have paid with Italian coins because they are not silver and none of them is worth more than a penny and a half. What's more they're so light they hardly make any sound at all. You *must* have paid him in foreign coins. You might have had some left over from the customs but you wouldn't have a whole pocket full. So I went to your room and found a pile of silver in your handkerchief drawer. What's more, they were new coins. They came directly from a roll and the roll came from Mrs. Sheridan's purse!"

He had caught her wrist. His fingers would not use pressure but she felt the strength in his wrist. She was a prisoner not of force but of the threat of force.

"Now listen. For one day you're going to forget everything you've seen, everything you've heard, and everything you've read. You will have a drink with the others now. In a little while you will have dinner. Then you'll go upstairs and get into bed, where you'll stay until noon tomorrow. If you can't sleep take something to read. But you won't come out of your room before and you won't speak of this to anyone. Say you're sick, if you like. But *don't do anything!*"

She looked steadily into his eyes. "I think you must tell me what will happen if I don't."

"There's no possibility of that. You understand? No possibility of your disobeying. You will do exactly what I say." The pressure tightened on her wrist—not enough to be painful but merely to emphasize. "You will stay in your room and let no one in."

"And you intend to make me?"

"I *will* make you." The hand tightened a fraction more. The blood was throbbing in her fingers. "There is no question of that."

She did not struggle but she put all of her resistance into her voice. "And I am telling you I will *not* let you do what you're planning. No matter what happens to me, you won't!"

There were needles of pain in her fingers. "Idiot! Don't you realize . . ."

The door opened and the pain stopped as though a switch had been turned. William stepped away from her, toward the newcomer. "Ah, Mr. Sims. We were beginning to wonder if you were coming. Will you have the usual? I expect Massimo left everything here. Mr. Voltor will be down soon. One moment, I'll ring for the hot water . . ."

In a second he had changed from an arrogant male to a slightly unctuous young man seeking favors from his betters. Celia was perfectly certain now that he was a murderer—but more than that, she had begun to realize, he was an actor.

Mr. Voltor and Mr. Sims sat at either side of Celia at the dinner table and glared across her plate as though they were amorous, not monetary, rivals. William was lavish with his usual pointless conversation, designed to nag them into some form of sociability.

"You spoke of Africa today, Mr. Voltor. Have you lived there?"

Henry looked annoyed, but his voice was soft with respect. "Good heavens, no. Never seen them."

"Them?" William leaned forward. A few grains of salt were balanced on a crystal salt spoon. Mr. Simms scowled past Celia.

"Colonies." Henry snapped a bread stick decisively.

"But didn't you mention Marrakech? I believe it was Marrakech." He sprinkled the salt in his soup.

"Ah—yes." He chewed on the shattered end of the bread stick as though it were a duty.

"Then you have been there?"

"No—some day, perhaps."

William turned to Anson. "Have you, Mr. Sims?"

"Have I what?" He was furiously wiping his knife with a napkin.

"Been to Marrakech—in North Africa?"

"Certainly not."

William considered this and nodded. "It must be fascinating," he said, letting his eyes pause for a moment as they met Celia's.

"Why?" Anson dipped his spoon gingerly into the clear soup.

"The gambling." William smiled knowingly at Henry Voltor. "I wonder why it is that gambling always seems more attractive in the south?"

"Does it?" Sims said.

William continued to watch Henry. "Not at all like the north, is it? The further south you go the more you *feel* like gambling. You take chances you would never have dreamed of at home. Do you agree, sir?"

Henry grunted. "I don't see that that's got anything to do with it."

"You don't? I should have thought you'd be the first to see. England, for instance. Now a person would never go to England to gamble, would he? If he wanted to gamble he'd leave England and go south. That's true, isn't it?"

Mr. Voltor sat precisely before his plate like a good child in a nursery. Celia noticed that he puckered his mouth when he ate. His lips reminded her of an overly hygienic nanny. He put down his spoon and said, "Very likely."

"Don't you think so, Mr. Sims? One generally leaves home and goes to some exotic place to gamble, wouldn't you say?"

Anson had been watching Henry. He turned quickly

now and said. "I know nothing of the methods of adventurers." He crumbled an inch of bread stick into his soup. " 'He that is greedy of gain troubleth his own house; but he that hateth gifts shall live.' Proverbs, fifteen, twenty-seven."

Again William caught Celia's eye. His smile frightened her. His teeth, she noticed, were very white, like those of an animal.

"But that's just the point. Most gamblers aren't adventurers. I'm sure of that—at any rate not professional adventurers. They are ordinary people. Like you—or Mr. Voltor—or myself."

Anson mumbled through a mouthful of softened crumbs. "I don't approve of gambling."

"Hear! Hear!" Henry's ears grew bright red, as though he were somehow embarrassed by his own bitterness, or at least by his show of feeling.

Mr. Sims glared past Celia. "May I ask what was the meaning of that, please?"

Voltor looked down at the table and toyed with his fork. "An American's unmannerly self-righteousness may be exceeded by his care to use phrases he imagines are polite."

Anson half rose. "I've had enough of your insults, sir!" His gaunt face strove to show anger and stopped short at petty rage. A kind of Abraham Lincoln *manqué*, Celia thought.

The color had spread from Henry's ears to his temples. He continued to play with his fork. "I shan't argue with you."

"That's enough!" William's voice stung like a ringmaster's whip. Both men looked at him. Celia felt that they were frightened also.

"We were speaking of gambling," the young man continued, softly. "Almost everyone gambles at one time or another, whether he approves of it or not." He stared relentlessly at Mr. Sims. "But amateur gamblers take too many chances. They are cautious all their lives and then —once—they lose everything."

"Lose?" Anson's sturdy chin showed a faint tremor.

"Exactly." William glanced at Massimo, who disappeared into the serving pantry. "Not all amateurs, of course. Not those who take the trouble to turn the odds in their favor. They sometimes do very well." He nodded to Henry. "Isn't that true, Mr. Voltor?"

Henry lay his spoon in his plate and touched a napkin to his dry lips. "I can't say," he replied.

The young man suddenly took four quarters from his pocket and put them on the table before Celia. "Very well. Here's a dollar. Suppose it represents a million— or five million—and you . . ." he looked solemnly at each of them ". . . both have a chance to win it."

Celia stared at the money. Shiny new quarters. His strong fingers caressed them.

"Think of five million—or ten. A fortune worth any possessions you choose, or security, or freedom—whatever you want! You may win it or lose it. Can you imagine what that means?" William's eyes reflected silver.

She wanted to reach out and take one of the quarters, just to make sure. Brand new. The date would give him away. Why had he taken them? Why be clever in every big thing and foolish in a small one? Both Mr. Sims and Mr. Voltor were watching the coins, like birds caught by the eyes of a snake.

"Do you understand? You may have ten million dollars or you may have nothing. You needn't lift a finger. This money is going to one of you, but . . ." He cut the sentence off sharp.

Anson breathed a husky, "Yes?"

"You need *me* to intercede."

Henry patted his glistening forehead.

"I can guarantee the money for one of you. But which one?" He picked up the quarters and let them fall on the table. One rolled next to Celia. "Remember—ten million. Which one shall I give it to?" As she was about to pick up the quarter William reached across the table and took it.

"Now, one of you realizes how much is at stake. He offers me a quarter. I have twenty-five percent of the ten million. He has the rest. Isn't that so, Mr. Sims?"

Anson shook his head, weakly. He glanced at Henry from the corner of his eye.

"But the *other* hears about it." William turned to Henry. "And he offers me half. Half is still not so bad, is it, Mr. Voltor?" William suddenly picked up two of the quarters and tossed them before Henry's plate.

Anson Sims was rigid. The veins in his neck were like wires. "You evil . . . !"

"*Ah, benissimo!*" William joyfully greeted the footman. He was carrying a silver tray laden with cold roast meats, artichoke hearts, pickled string beans, baked chilled tomatoes, trussed birds and lobster under aspic. Massimo came behind with a sweating decanter of rosé wine. "*È fresco, il vino?*"

"*Si signore. Freschissimo.*"

Celia was afraid the old man would have a stroke.

"By the way," William said, as the footman set the tray on the sideboard and began to take off the heavy soup dishes. "You may be interested to know that Mr. Fox has executed his will."

Henry Voltor placed both hands on the table and drew his breath. His face was suffused with a faint, holy light. A pilgrim first catching sight of the Holy Land.

"Yes?" Anson was dead white, turning yellow.

"Everything's in order," William said, briskly. "Who'd like some of the birds? They're stuffed with Mr. Fox's white truffle dressing. He says that civilization is the process of removing the activities of human life known as "cooking" and "medicine" from the hands of women."

Henry let his breath out softly. "You mean he has named . . . ?"

"Well, no. He hasn't named anyone yet. He couldn't bring himself to leave either of his old friends out of his will."

Celia saw Mr. Sims bend slightly, as though he had just put down a great weight.

"At my suggestion he left the name blank. I'm afraid the poor old gentleman no longer trusts his own judgment. He insists that I . . ."

Anson reached cautiously for his water glass. "He insists . . . ?" He took two restorative sips.

"He wants me to choose for him. *I* am supposed to tell him which of his two friends is most worthy to be his heir."

Henry shook his head as the silver tray paused at his left. His mouth was like a rubber band. "I wonder," he said, picking up the quarters, "what would happen to your players if they simply forgot about you and had a chat between themselves." He looked directly at Anson, daring the man to find distaste in his expression.

"Because," William said, heaping his plate high, "I might arrange it so that neither of you won. Also, you don't trust each other. You never will; you're too much alike. You must remember . . ." he picked up one of the remaining quarters and tossed it before Mr. Sims. ". . . that even a quarter of the money involved would be considered an enormous fortune by most people."

Celia nibbled at her lobster. She could not bear to eat one of the little birds. She had stopped listening. It was too confusing and she was tired. William could have no reason for this foolishness, unless he hoped to establish some kind of alibi for himself. She already knew that neither one of the old men would inherit the money. The important thing was that Mr. Fox *would* die—soon—unless she warned him.

William did not leave her after dinner. He reminded both Sims and Voltor that he would be in his room all evening, then he took her arm and accompanied her upstairs. She thought, for a second, of calling for help. But there was no one to call but the two old men whom her captor held prisoner even more firmly than he held her. The servants would not be able to understand her and, anyway, would probably obey him. The only one to ask for help was the one she was determined to help. She said nothing when he took the keys of her room and the adjoining one. He ordered her again not to leave until tomorrow noon, and then made the order superfluous by locking her in.

She went to her bed and lay down. The tiny mirrors in the ceiling caught up her reflection and multiplied it by the million. It occurred to her, almost with relief, that she was helpless. If she had disobeyed and run to warn

Mr. Fox, William would have killed her. She was sure of that. All she had to do now was to keep quiet until tomorrow noon and she would be perfectly safe. Furthermore, William would have a great deal of money . . .

Celia stared at the mirrored ceiling. She was a sea being drawn up by the moon. A huge coin hanging in the dark sky, drawing her, drawing. . . . She had never felt like this before. Money had never meant much to her. But now the thought of going back to New York and standing in a little book shop, drafty in winter and stifling in summer, hour after hour on tender feet, was more than she could bear. She *liked* nice things. Mr. Fox himself had told her not to choose poverty, if she could avoid it. Well, now she could, simply by staying here in her room until tomorrow noon. And Death would take care of everything. Everything . . . her mind drifted to more comfortable thoughts.

How many reflections of herself flashed on the ceiling! Back and forth, from one mirror to another, returning endlessly. And in each image she was no more than—Celia. Celia Johns, a girl she normally referred to as "you" when she was speaking to herself. If she got close enough to the mirrors she could probably see the tiny scar on her temple where she had fallen on a rake when she was a girl. Or she could find the mark from chicken pox on her cheek which she had got for disobeying her grandmother's orders not to scratch. Everything she had ever done left some mark to be repeated, now, infinitely. Who was she then? Who was this "you"? Was she anything but the sum of all the accidents, the decisions, the moments of cowardice and bravery, of her life? Was she a person to whom things happened or was she instead the simple total of what *did* happen?

Celia suddenly got up. How could *she*, who knew death in others so well, be deceived when it came to her? Did she want to grow old like Mrs. Sheridan, afraid to sleep or wake? Afraid to see or hear? People did not die first with their bodies. That was the last thing that went. The important battles took place long before. You did not have to be afraid, as long as you fought. For it was the fighting itself that kept you from being one of the walking dead. She knew, now, that she would warn Mr. Fox if she had to break through the ceiling . . .

She began to smile. Of course. Why not through the ceiling? She walked directly across the room and opened the door of the dumb-waiter.

CHAPTER EIGHTEEN

Cecil Fox placed his hourglass alongside the enamel clock his dead guest had given him, pushed the tables next to the walls, switched the bed around to the side, rolled up the fur rugs which spotted the floor, and removed his shoes. Then he set a record on the spinning table of a portable phonograph, examined the door again to make sure it was locked, and began to move around the room. As he glided past the clocks on the mantel, he snatched a perspiring glass from between them and continued to circle, taking a sip or two before he put it down. The night was excluded by thick, brocade curtains. From time to time Cecil passed through a door into his sitting room, holding himself as lightly as two hundred and seven pounds can be held, spinning in defiance of age and the laws of nature, running around a giant Persian vase on tiptoe, and returning to his starting place. He was indulging himself in the only vice he had which was secret. On the brilliant stage of his imagination he was dancing.

When the record was played he turned it over and started again. His eyes were shining with the fierce light of creation. Now *that* was exceptional, that step. Untutored, of course. He's never had a lesson in his life. Did you know, he's never had a lesson . . . ? But astonishing! So light on his feet. He does what ordinary professional dancers wouldn't dare do. Look! Look at that leap! Stupendous. Ah, the stage lost a great talent in him. They say he's over sixty. You'd never believe he was a day past thirty-five—a day past forty . . . astonishing . . .

Cecil stopped. He turned toward the rear, to the left of the bed. There, crouched literally within the wall, on the main shelf of the dumb-waiter, clinging to a heavy rope, was a girl.

He strode to the phonograph and shut it off. His manner was stiff and unnaturally pompous. His face and neck were a rich burgundy. He spun around. "Well—are you going to sit there all night?"

Celia's voice came faintly. "I—I can't get out."

Cecil scowled. "How long have you been there?"

"You don't understand. Help me. If I let go I'll fall. And I can't move, without . . ." The rope slipped in her hands and she dropped an inch.

"I ought to let you."

"Please!"

He went to the dumb-waiter and reached inside. "All right. I've got it. Get out, fast! Who told you to come up here and spy? Who in Sam Hill sent you up here, huh?"

Celia climbed out, trying to keep her dress decently below her knees. "No one. It was my idea. I had to come."

The old man pushed the dumb-waiter button angrily. It didn't work. "Broke! Blast you, you broke the motor. Now it'll have to be worked by hand. What am I going to do for breakfast? You come up here and interrupt my —my exercises and tear my house apart to boot."

Celia began to massage her arms. "Those weren't exercises. You were dancing."

"They were too," Cecil sputtered. "Doctor's orders." He banged the dumb-waiter door shut and went to rescue his drink.

The girl followed him. "I saw you. You were dancing for fun. I know, I do it myself. Why are you ashamed of it?"

He turned back to her, but before he could speak a wave of misery drenched his anger. "I'm ashamed, honey, because I can't dance well. I'd give everything I have to dance well. I was *born* to, I know. Except I was born in the wrong body." He looked down sadly and took a long swallow from his drink. His white robe was twisted. Celia noticed that he had little clumps of hair growing from the tops of his toes.

"I used to think the same thing. Except I was sorry I wasn't born ugly."

The old man began to cheer up. "You sure weren't, dolly."

"The point is, it doesn't take much to make a person look either ugly *or* beautiful if that's what he really wants. And you could probably have learned to dance, too . . ."—she looked down at his stomach—"if you didn't like other things better."

He beckoned to her and they went into the sitting room. He showed her to a chair and patted her arm lingeringly as she sat down. "Why did you *have* to come?" he said, pleased by her choice of words.

She stared at him coldly. "Not for the reason you think."

He looked shocked. "Good Heavens—you don't imagine that I . . ."

"Yes."

"Well then, why?" he said, irritably.

She clenched her hands. "It's so hard to believe," she said, at last.

"What is?" Cecil went to a green and silver cabinet and removed a large box.

"That's why I'm here," she said, slowly. "I have to tell you. I could let it go, but if anything were to happen to you I'd know it was my fault."

He held the box before her. It was made of cherry-wood, dyed only with age and rubbed to a fine polish. The lid popped open and three tiers of assorted chocolates were slowly extended to her as the machinery set off a tinkling serenade. "What would happen to me," he said, smiling.

She took one from the top layer, capped with bright green *marzapane*. "You might be killed."

He laughed and took a chocolate for himself. "We'll have to eat these in a week or they'll go bad," he said, happily. "You must come more often."

"You don't believe me?"

"Well, a person *might* always be killed, I suppose."

"But I swear you will be, if you don't listen to me." Her very earnestness seemed to disqualify her.

"Try the ones on the bottom. They have gold centers." He held out the box again.

"I tell you there is a murderer in this house. I know!"

"You know?" He mocked her voice, faintly annoyed.

She took a chocolate. Cecil snapped the box shut and dropped it on a table fashioned like a huge shell.

"Yes, I have proof."

He drew up a chair. "Tell me what proof, dolly. Tell everything to your uncle Sturdivant."

"Sturdivant?"

"I'm afraid my name is Sturdivant Cecil Fox Sheridan. You might as well know everything, sweety. As soon as I was old enough to know better I dropped Sturdivant like a hot rock. Sheridan was my father's name and I didn't like him very much. So when I was a kid I adopted Fox—that was my mother's. Later I used Sheridan for certain adventures until the old bat you worked for grabbed it, along with a bankfull of my money. What proof, honey?"

"The pills. They weren't . . ." She looked down at the candy she had bitten into. "Why, the centers *are* gold."

"Only a little in the paste. For show. They come from that joint on the Rue Saint Honoré. The pills weren't what . . . ?"

"But they must cost a fortune!" She chewed the second half as though it would break her teeth.

"But easier to digest than most fortunes. What was the matter with the pills, baby?"

"Nothing. That's just the point. They were harmless. I mean they were made of sugar."

He leaned forward and placed a confidential hand on her knee. "Slow down, sweet. Start from the beginning. We've got all night." He looked at his new chronometer. "Ten o'clock, Sunday night, April twentieth. Good Lord, you'd think they wouldn't bother to tell you what day it was. At least not Sunday. I'd know it any time, wouldn't you?"

Celia nodded. She was already feeling calmer. Things couldn't possibly be as urgent as they seemed. "Yes," she said, noticing his nostalgic smile.

He looked down at his naked feet and wiggled his toes.

"My mother used to come to my room and tell me a story on Sunday nights. It was the kind of story that never finished. About a man named Mr. Moley, who had a sack full of magic tricks. He could use one each week to get out of the trouble he was in the week before. Then one week—he didn't."

"He didn't?"

"I'm sorry. Go on. Start from the beginning." He gestured to her impatiently. "He didn't because my mother died. I thought the next week he would . . ."

"I'm sorry."

His eyes flashed. "The hell you are. Go on."

"Very well." She folded her hands in her lap. "I went to your library just before dinner."

He grinned. "So you've caught the fox at last."

"Yes—and now I am trying to save his life."

"You want me to suggest some ways, honey?"

"I guessed when you were talking about the Elizabethans out there in the garden. Before then, when you called Mrs. Sheridan 'Old Crow,' I almost recognized the play. First a fox, then a crow. Even William—Proudfly —Fly. I don't know how you had such astonishing luck, or is that his name?"

Cecil pulled his cigar case from his pajama pocket. "The fact is, I was going to hire a fellow named Mapes but I got Willy's letter at the last moment. I didn't even want an actor, but with a name like that I had to take him."

"It's too bad you didn't choose the other. William is a little too much of an actor." She paused while he lighted his cigar.

"Go on."

"He knew Ben Jonson's *Volpone*, naturally. Even I

should have remembered that Volpone simply means Fox."

"Big Fox," Cecil corrected.

"It would have been difficult for him not to recognize the story. Volpone was an old man living in Venice who let it be known through his servant, a certain Mosca, or Fly, that he was dying and about to make his will. Three friends rushed to his side to speed him on his way. The parallel was perfectly obvious."

"Except for the part about my being an old man, dolly. All right, so he guessed."

"Let me finish. In the play, after Volpone takes everything he can from his friends he decides to get rid of them and he tells his servant to announce that he is dead. When Mosca reads the will the 'friends' discover that *he* has inherited everything. Mosca stops playing the parasite and orders the three scavengers out of the house while Volpone hides behind a curtain and watches the fun."

"Now you can't say it won't be fun, honey. Want to watch?"

Celia looked at him solemnly. "Unless you listen to me you won't be *there* to see what happens."

Cecil clamped his cigar in his mouth. "Go on."

"You know that in the play Mosca also turns on his master and locks *him* out."

"Of course, dolly, but I had my own ideas about the end."

"Obviously—especially as Volpone is finally caught and thrown into a dungeon so that he might at last grow as ill as he pretended to be. And Mosca was sent to the galleys for life."

Cecil stared at the ceiling dreamily. "It might even be

worth it to see Willy dragged off to the galleys. Just for cheating at cards."

Celia paused. "Cheating? I don't . . ."

"You don't believe it?"

"No—other things, yes, but not that."

"What other things?"

She set her mouth. "What I'm trying to tell you is that William was going to change the ending of your little play also. I have proof that he murdered Mrs. Sheridan. Until this afternoon I didn't understand why. He seemed to have no motive. Now I realize that she was the one person who could have interfered with his plans. If she could prove that she was your common-law wife she might inherit from you no matter whom you had named in your will."

The old man was amused. "You don't mean the kid wants to see *me* die?"

"Exactly. I suppose you were going to follow the play and send your 'friends' away as Volpone did?"

"Oh sure. That's the whole point."

"And William is going to inherit?"

"You sure you don't want to watch?"

"No. And unless you are careful you will *really* be dead when he reads the will."

The old man chuckled but his eyes had suddenly grown uneasy.

"When were you going to stage the final scene?"

"Tomorrow morning. I have the will all ready."

She looked toward the bedroom. "Is the door locked . . . ?"

He laughed. "Sure dolly, we're snug as two pips in a pippin."

"It's not funny. I wish you'd see that. Somehow he'll

try to kill you tonight. I know it. You've told everybody you're near death. I expect even the servants would back up the story as much as necessary if he got to them tonight. In the meantime he has two excellent witnesses who will tell the police that you expected to die within days. They'll be furious, but they won't deny that. There will be no investigation. You'll be given a simple burial ceremony. William will go away, arrange with his lawyers to liquidate your estate and wait for his money. Don't you see how easy it is? You've done all the work for him."

Cecil was frowning. "You still haven't given me the proof that he *did* kill Mrs. Sheridan. After all, what's the matter with my other guests? They have motives also."

"They aren't the type," she said, confidently.

He snickered. "I see you've met a lot of murderers."

Celia was obstinate. "If I show you that William did kill the old lady will you admit that he intends to murder you next?"

"I suppose I'd have to."

"All right. At least you'll listen. You see, I can pay for my keep after all." She told him of Mrs. Sheridan's habit of waking up at night and demanding an extra pill. From the very beginning of her job, she said, she had given a sugar tablet as the second dose. "It made no difference. She just wanted to *control* sleep."

"I know," Cecil said. "And every other thing. One of the reasons she took to traveling around was that she couldn't tell the weather what to do if she stayed in one place."

"William was the only one I told about the second pill. You see how he used that? He went to her room, raised her up in bed while she was half asleep and gave her enough to stun her. Then in a few minutes he could increase the dose to any size he wanted. He must have brought sleeping medicine—there was a pharmacy just outside the movie—because he couldn't be sure of finding mine. But when he saw the bottle in her bag he emptied it and left it beside her bed. That way it looked like suicide or an accident."

Mr. Fox shook his head. "That doesn't explain how he could be with you in a movie and murdering the old girl at the same time."

Celia told him about the movie. "I remember William leaving his seat at the beginning of the second half. I didn't notice when he came back because I was watching him so closely on the screen, but it could have been half an hour or forty-five minutes. You see, he was not only sure that I wouldn't interrupt him in Mrs. Sheridan's room, but if he was lucky he also had an alibi. I couldn't *swear* he didn't come back to his seat five minutes after he left.

"Then the coins. He paid the gondolier who took us home with them. I didn't notice then but the bill must have been several dollars and it would have taken a whole sack of Italian coins to make that much. When I realized, later, that the only thing missing from Mrs. Sheridan's purse was change, I knew William had taken it. I can't understand why, but he did. It was stupid, and he certainly is not stupid."

Cecil had begun to pull harder on his cigar. The little sitting room was clouded. "You're sure the pills were harmless?"

"Absolutely sure. I used my last real one when she went to bed."

"I see." He gnawed the end of his cigar. "Of course you haven't exactly proved your point. Assuming she was killed, it might still have been anyone in the house . . . or out of it. It might even have been me, you know." A wisp of smoke rose past his eyes.

She shook her head, impatiently. "Just because she was your common-law wife? That's silly. Lots of men are married to women they don't like. Without a stronger motive than that, or at least a stronger feeling, they don't become murderers. No—it was obviously William. Of course I know there's a difference between a reasonable suspicion and confirmation in court. Only the police could get the kind of proof you're asking for. But I *have* shown you that Mrs. Sheridan was probably murdered and that William was almost certainly in her room at about the time of her death. I don't know how he did kill her. An autopsy would show. The important thing is that he tried to make it seem that she died by taking the pills which she had in her purse. And I can *swear* that they were harmless."

Cecil stood up and went to the Persian vase. "You think I'll be his next victim, then?" He dropped in the butt of his cigar.

"What other reason did he have for killing a defenseless old woman?"

"Dolly, that woman was no more defenseless than a Bengal tiger."

She ignored him. ". . . because it would be useless to kill you if she were still alive. You'll be the next!"

He came back to her chair and offered her the box of chocolates again. "Just one more thing . . ." The lid popped open and the music summoned.

"Yes?" She chose a candy from the middle row.

"You were supposed to have reported to the police that Mrs. Sheridan's death was an accident. Why?"

Celia felt herself blushing. "Because—I was protecting him."

Cecil chose one of the gold-centered chocolates for himself and put the box down, open. "And you aren't, any longer?"

She wiped her fingers with her handkerchief. "That hasn't anything to do with this. You can't bring back the dead. But I couldn't let you be killed also."

He nodded, slowly. He seemed tired. "I suppose you told *him* everything you suspected. You wouldn't think of doing anything sensible like minding your business and saving your own neck. What happened, did you fall for him?"

"I said that hasn't got anything to do with it." She quickly took another chocolate. "Of course I told him."

"Go on, kid. Eat some more. There's only one thing wrong with your looks. There isn't quite enough of you." He stared directly at a part of her body which had never, until then, been openly stared at. "What'd he say?"

She squeezed her handkerchief into a ball. "He told me to stay in my room until noon tomorrow."

"Very sound advice."

"But can't you see? He didn't want me to warn you!"

Cecil nodded. "I see, exactly."

She jumped up. Her handkerchief dropped to the floor. "Aren't you going to do something?"

He took her arm and led her toward the bedroom. "Very little." He stood aside and let her go through the door first.

"But why? Even if you left the house that would be enough. You don't know what he is."

Cecil led her to the fireplace, before the enamel clock. "Yes I do, now. It's all because of that damn name. I should have hired Mapes. These lousy actors are all scene-stealers."

She gripped his arm. It was surprisingly muscular. "He's after your money. He'll do anything. Why won't you believe me!"

The old man began to giggle. It started as something like a bird call and gathered volume and resonance as it went on. His fact took on the unhealthy color of good raspberry ice. When he had finished he threw his arms around her with careless intimacy and kissed her soundly underneath the left ear. "Oh dolly, you're the best."

"But . . ."

He raised a hand to stop her. "Look, honey. Look at this clock. It measures time. But do you think it gives a damn whether it measures good or bad time? No—it doesn't know anything about that. But *we* do, you and me. Huh? We're clocks, too, but when we come across some good time we slow down. You know, to sop it up. Right now I'm slowed down. Ten minutes from now is maybe ten years. Don't think I don't appreciate your coming to warn me. I'll think about it in a year or two, I promise. In the meantime why don't you go back to your room. Do what Willy tells you."

Celia began to object again, but he shook his head. "Very well," she said, "I'll go back. But I know that you won't be alive tomorrow. I'm sorry, but I *know* it. If you don't help yourself no one else can."

"I'll try to remember the maxim, sweety. Now get the hell out." He walked to the door.

"I—I can only go back the way I came. My room is locked. William . . ."

"Bright boy. All right," he said, turning toward the dumb-waiter. "If you can come up alone I suppose we can get you down together. And Lord love you, girl, go to bed and stay there!"

When she was safely down Cecil locked the dumb-waiter door, poured himself a stiff drink and turned on the phonograph again. He began to dance.

"They say he's sixty-five." "No!" "He doesn't look a day over . . ." *Last night this reviewer was privileged to see . . . will never be equalled!*

He continued to circle after the music had stopped. His arms were limp and his feet dragged. His robe fell open, revealing a ponderous belly. Even his face at last betrayed his age. He stumbled and came to a stop. Slowly, he sank to the floor, clasping his knees. The needle clicked around the empty center grooves of the record. Then Marie Antoinette's clock struck the half hour and Cecil looked up at its face. Pierrot spun. The courtier dallied. He turned to the gaunt hourglass, building its hill of gold. The old man began to beat on the floor with his open hand. He was chuckling.

CHAPTER NINETEEN

Celia woke a few minutes before dawn. A pale light melted through her shutters, threatening the sweet lies of sleep. At the bottom of every day was this eerie undercoat of grey which the sun first spread on the world before it added its stronger colors. But there was something more. Why had she waked? She was never up at this hour. And the dream itself was somehow too nice, like the toy offered a child before it is dragged into an operating room. She looked from the window and saw a man standing over her bed.

She didn't move. His hands hung loosely over her. She saw a finger twitch and noticed that the cuffs showed, as though he were reaching forward. They were strong hands, as she already knew. There was no point in trying to escape them by struggling.

"Why?" she said aloud, keeping her voice as clear and precise as possible.

The hands retreated suddenly. "I wanted to speak to you."

She still did not move. "You know I went to see him, don't you."

"Yes. That was very foolish."

"I told you I would. I had to."

"I should have thought of the dumb-waiter."

"And now?" She held her breath.

There was a long pause. "The old man is dead," William said.

"I know."

"You think I killed him?"

The light was beginning to increase. His body was like a figure in a photographic negative, stolid, outlined in black. She would never see anything more, she realized. This day was only a threat. It would stop before the light touched his face, or hers. It was the day of her death.

"I know you did." She wasn't afraid.

He took a single step toward her bed. Celia closed her eyes. Suddenly she was back again in the homely middle western graveyard, following her grandmother down aisles of headstones to one beside her sleeping parents which read:

"YOU"

CHAPTER TWENTY

" '. . . being of sound mind, do hereby declare . . .' " William's voice droned through the introductory part of the will, savoring the monotony. He was standing before the green and gold cabinet in Mr. Fox's sitting room. Before him were Anson Sims and Henry Voltor. The latter was seated cross-legged on a fragile loveseat and looked like an advertisement for British shoes. Anson had chosen a chair which sat as straightly as he did.

" 'I have instructed my secretary to read my will in the presence of my body, less as a sentimental gesture than as a reminder to all of you of your approach to death. No matter how you squirm you come closer every day.' "

"Ridiculous farce!" Henry snapped. "It is unnecessary to read us the details of a will which by now hardly concerns either one of us. Let's come to the essentials immediately."

William cleared his throat discreetly. "I am sorry, but I have been instructed to read it all." He resumed: " 'I would like to say, with the customary insincerity of this sort of document, that the choice of an heir has been a painful one; but I cannot. It was one of the most heart-warming actions of my life. The man who will inherit my possessions is . . .' "

Henry's foot jerked in the air. "I don't believe it," he

said, glaring at Anson. "You jolly well didn't offer him *ninety* percent."

Sims looked shocked. "Did *you?*"

"We could still agree to . . ."

William raised his voice. "Gentlemen! Please." He looked severely toward the door of the bedroom. From where the two men sat they could see the corner of the bed on which the corpse was lying. He continued reading:

" '. . . worth very little, but he is vastly superior to those I have rejected. I realize that in making the choice I have sown the seeds of discomfort, perhaps even misery, in two worthless lives. I have administered justice with the heavy hand which is usually reserved for injustice. In short, my decision was not only easily made, it was brilliantly correct.' "

The two men shifted uncomfortably. Henry brought out his handkerchief and touched his temples. There was a forewarning of disaster in his eyes. Anson sat like a stone.

" 'Therefore my will only slightly concerns the man here named. It is written primarily to those I have disinherited.' "

William paused. His two listeners did not move. They seemed to have grown physically smaller—and older.

" 'I'll tell you what you are, both of you. You, Sims, are an eager pauper and you, Voltor, are a complacent nobody. One of you was born with a great fortune and the other with a great name and in nearly a lifetime you have almost succeeded in erasing both. You *want* to be poor, you *want* to be undistinguished. What you two call thrift and exclusiveness are really poverty and obscurity. That's what you want and that's what you've got. You haven't got the cream to be what you were born. One of you measures his social distinction by the cut of his shirt and the address of his club and the other counts his wealth by the number of months he can continue using one razor blade. Was there ever anything more ignominious? More beggarly?

" 'And yet you are greedy. You want *more* money to waste and *other* names to hide. Just because you've made such a puling mess you think you have the right to do it again. And if you'd withered this chance you would want others. Your eyes are starving for joints and you can't swallow milk toast. You haven't the bowels for a penny's worth of living and you want ten millions.

" 'I knew your declarations of friendship were as hollow as paper hats. You came running for the money, of course. But you are wrong if you think I minded that. What I couldn't bear was your *contempt* for money. For all that you traveled thousands of miles to get it, you had no real idea of its worth and you never will have. For you, money is a crutch. It keeps you up, makes you important to yourselves, supports your rotten little notions. And that is why you wanted *my* money.

" 'Now this malady is usually attributed to the rich, who often have more than they can use and want more than they have. But, in fact, *it is people like you who give the rest of us a bad name.* You, with your niggardly habits, and appetites for which you have no stomachs. In the name of all riches and hard-won distinction I therefore disown you. However, I am pleased to leave you the following:

" 'My old friend Anson Sims is to be sent, airmail, the backs of all my used envelopes, every shred of grocery string to be found in the house, the rubber bands, the pins, the stubs of pencils, and any old stamps without stickum.

" 'An agency in the city of London will be hired to place prominent ads in all daily papers to the effect that a certain Angelo Brutto, a rich Milanese office equipment manufacturer, wishes to be put in touch with Mr. Henry Voltor, whom he believes to be his natural son. I leave this to my heir to accomplish over Mr. Voltor's objections.

" 'With the performance of these two works of vengeance, my secretary, Mr. William Fieramosca, has fulfilled all the conditions of my will and may enjoy my wealth in the manner which most pleases him.' "

William laid the will on the cabinet. Without speaking he looked toward the bedroom door. The two old men turned and watched also. Their faces were numb, almost gentle, with acceptance. "And that fulfills my promise," William said, slowly.

"Promise?" Anson's face seemed ready to crack open.

"I had a job to do. It's done." He turned around and reached into the cabinet. "And now I'd like to explain a few things to you."

"I think you've explained enough already," said Henry; wearily.

"There should be . . . Yes, here it is." He took the cherrywood box from the cabinet. "A sort of peace offering," he said, smiling.

Anson looked pained. "You knew—all along?"

"Yes. But you don't understand."

The gaunt old face clouded with ineffectual hate. "I understand everything. Everything."

William held the box out to Voltor. The lid popped open and chiming music filled the room. "No—you do not. You see, the old man was broke."

He looked down. The box was empty.

CHAPTER TWENTY-ONE

William shrugged and put the box back in the cabinet. "Funny, there were a lot yesterday."

"Broke?" Anson said, as though he were waking from a dream. "But you said . . ."

"I didn't know it myself until yesterday. I should have guessed at the end of the first week when my salary wasn't paid. He was flat broke. I don't think he had enough even for a train ticket out, if his plan failed." He glanced again toward the bedroom.

"He was hardly in any condition to take a train," Henry said.

"He was in perfect condition. You'll see in a moment. The police will be here soon and I want to tell you a few things before they come. Not that I think you deserve an explanation but I'm feeling a little remorseful. I deliberately put the screws on you last night because I knew I'd never have another chance to play a part like this. You'd have to be actors to know what I mean. But I took you through the last scene this morning for *his* sake. He was listening, I know."

"What about the money I lent him?" Sims jumped from his chair.

Henry looked startled. "The money *you* lent . . ." He stopped, swamped by a wave of understanding.

"We'll go to the police!"

William smiled. He seemed tired. "The police are coming. But I'm afraid you're out of luck. Let me tell you what happened."

Henry's eyes were wide with fear. "It wasn't mine," he moaned. "I've got to pay it back. You *must* give it to me!"

Anson placed a hand on his shoulder. "I think," he said, with a quaver, "that we'd better listen. Perhaps there's something we can do . . ."

William took a chair. "Yes, it's best if you listen."

He reached into his pocket and took out a package of cigarettes. He hesitated, then threw them on the shell table and drew a cigar from his inner pocket. "First of all, you might as well know that I had been working for the old man a little more than a week before you came. I'm an actor, of sorts. I came to play a part." He lit a match and twirled the cigar in the flame.

"Never mind what the part was. It wouldn't mean anything to you anyway. It's enough to say that he pretended to be dying so he could fleece you. He expected you to come with presents and you did. I was surprised that you each brought a timepiece, but the old man explained that, as you were counting the hours to his death, it would be natural for your minds to turn in the same direction. He was very fond of your gifts. I know he would want me to tell you that."

Henry tried to be casual. "Of course, now that he has no use for them, I suppose . . ."

William shook his head. "I'm afraid you'll have a hard time getting them back. There are special circumstances . . ."

Anson spoke hesitantly. "You say he 'pretended' to be dying. Do you mean that Cecil was perfectly well?"

"Sound as a bell. I was supposed to read his will while he hid behind the door and listened. He expected 'a rare meal of laughter,' gentlemen."

Both Voltor and Sims turned slowly to the doorway.

"You needn't be afraid. Mr. Fox *intended* to eavesdrop on us. He wanted to see you squirm. But now he is quite dead."

"Then how *did* he die?" Henry said.

William prodded the shell table with his foot. "Let me go back to the beginning. As I say, I should have known that Mr. Fox was broke. There were other signs besides my missing salary. Look at this table. Look at this whole room, in fact. Does it seem like a man's? There aren't even any ash trays in it. That vase, the cabinet, the loveseat. It's all too delicate. Compare it with the furniture in the study, for example. And the pink and blue living rooms; do they seem like Cecil Fox's taste? The dining room is furnished for a big family. The dishes are heavy family dishes—not the sort of china he would have for himself.

"Then, almost half the rooms in this house are not furnished. Even the main apartment is bare. Not only was the old man broke but all the furniture here except for a few beds, some chairs in the reception room and an odd table or two, was rented. He chose the best he could find. I believe some of the things, especially in the study, once actually were his. But the house has obviously been pieced together in a hurry. As for the servants, after a while he could expect them to stick around if only to collect their back pay. You can make an investment of work as well as money.

"I don't think the old fraud even had any clothes, except for his fancy pajamas and robes. Nobody would buy *them.* He'd probably sold everything else to provision the house. The last time I saw him wear a suit was the day before you came. Massimo probably hocked it.

"As you see, and as the police have already informed me, I was making myself a party to extortion. But somehow you never think of a rich man as capable of extortion even when you catch him in the act. Also, I believed that all of you were wealthy and that these little games among millionaires weren't really to be taken seriously. If I had known the old man was broke I wouldn't have taken the job, even if he could have guaranteed my salary, which I needed. The question is hardly a moral one. Why should I make myself liable to arrest for a few hundred a week? The stakes were too low.

"Of course they were also too low for Cecil Fox. He might have wrung twenty or thirty thousand out of you with his story, but he would never get much more. And, as you know, he was a man made for 'much more' if anyone ever was. He had decided to kill one of you."

Both Voltor and Sims looked as though someone had fired a pistol behind their backs.

"Only one of you. If I had known at the start that he had no money I might even have guessed it—especially as I got to know the rather—unusual scope of his mind. He was going to make money in exactly the way all of you were hoping to. He intended to inherit it."

Henry interrupted cautiously. "I beg your pardon. It happens that the hourglass I brought has been in my family for many years and . . ."

William began to laugh. "You should never have got yourself mixed up in this, Voltor. You give up too easily. A couple of days ago you were shooting for millions. Now I could make you settle for your fare back."

His face glowed. "Absolutely not—I merely . . ."

"How do you mean, he intended to inherit it?" Anson said.

"As Mrs. Sheridan explained, she was the old gentleman's common-law wife. But when the phrase 'common-law wife' is used we forget that there is another one which necessarily accompanies it. There must also be a 'common-law husband.' Miss Johns told me that her employer had no heirs. Yet surely a husband, common-law or not, would be considered an heir, especially if he could prove that the old woman's money originally came from him. The suspicious circumstances of her death would never be taken into account as long as the Italian authorities had certified the death as accidental.

"We all assumed that nothing could be more repulsive to Mr. Fox than to discover after all these years that he had a wife—especially this one. But that is exactly why he arranged this elaborate farce. Under its cover he could murder his rich wife. While pretending to be, at the worst, an eccentric practical joker, he would earn himself several million dollars."

William stopped and tapped the ash of his cigar onto the floor with a proprietory air. "I say again, I should have foreseen a lot of this. When I began to suspect what was going on, it was too late. Friday night I took Miss Johns to the movies and at the intermission I called a friend of mine who works for a news agency in Rome. I asked him to check the financial status of Mr. Fox's three guests. I received a special delivery letter Sunday morning saying that you, Mr. Voltor, live on an adequate but rather shabby income which comes primarily from a family estate you rent to a plastics manufacturer. You, Mr. Sims, were once one of the wealthiest men in

America, but for nearly thirty years your affairs have been in chaos. You haggle over the money on the right hand side of the decimal point and would rather lose a million than allow your advisors taxi fare. My friend predicts that you will be destitute in another ten years. He says that Mrs. Sheridan, on the other hand, was loaded."

He stood up and looked around the room for an ash tray. At last he went to the window, pulled it open and threw the butt into the canal. He turned to the two old men. "Do you have any questions so far?"

Both retained a sullen silence.

"Very well. On Friday evening I told Mr. Fox that I wanted to go out. I was beginning to be suspicious. It's surprising how easily you can be suspicious when you haven't been paid. I had decided to call my friend in Rome, but I wanted to do it out of the house. He suggested that I take Miss Johns with me, which I did, thereby condemning Mrs. Sheridan to a quick and probably painless death. The police report shows a barbiturate present in her stomach. However, it was not the same type as that indicated on the label of the bottle found by her bed. It couldn't be traced. Barbiturates are sold without prescription in Italy."

Anson shook his head. "I don't believe that she could have been forced to take enough pills to kill her. There would have been a struggle."

"None at all. You forget that Mr. Fox had lived with the old woman. He knew her as well as anyone could. He knew, first of all, that she took sleeping medicine. She was nuts on sleep. I'm sure you've known people like that yourself. If they don't get a certain number of hours' sleep every night they go out of their minds with worry.

They can't wake up for ten minutes without going into a cold sweat that they won't get back to sleep. I don't know why—but the severe cases are nearly insane."

William came back to his chair. "Now Cecil Fox knew one other thing about the old lady that gave him the opening he wanted. He understood that she was a person who lived to give orders. She would do nothing for herself that could be done for her. Very well. He simply went into Miss Johns' room and made enough noise to wake the woman. She did exactly what he expected. She called for a sleeping pill. If she hadn't he could have gone out the other door and found some other way of killing her later. The rest was easy. It was dark. He knew the room perfectly. He walked to her bedside, handed her a double or triple strength sleeping capsule, gave her a glass of water and waited. In a few minutes he could repeat the procedure and give her as much as he wanted. And that was the end of her life. He had designed the murder for one woman and no other. It was a perfect custom fit."

He stopped and went to the bedroom door and listened. "I think I hear someone downstairs," he said. "I'll try to be quick."

Henry looked bewildered. "You said the police report showed barbiturates in her stomach. I thought they had listed it as an accidental death?"

"That comes in a moment. Before the old man left Mrs. Sheridan's room he did something remarkably foolish. To understand it you must remember the sort of person he was. He stole all the coins from her bag. You see, he was a gambler, not only in large matters but in small. Specifically, he was a poker player. He pulled me into a game the first day I was in the house. The only cash he had in the world was a box of American coins, which I won from him, seldom honestly. I used to be a shill in a Reno gambling club and I have never seen such blatant cheating in my life. It was all I could do to keep winning. He was furious.

"Of course it was idiotic to take anything from the old lady's purse. Especially money, which would be checked first. But this was small change; he didn't even think of it as money and he already considered all of Mrs. Sheridan's property his own. He would as easily have taken a pack of matches. As a matter of fact it did escape the police's attention, because coins are used so seldom in Italy. But Miss Johns knew.

"Cecil Fox was certain to inherit an estate of several million. He also had a scheme to fleece you two out of enough money to last him—in his usual magnificent style—until the final disposition of his wife's money in the U. S. courts. He had all he wanted but he *didn't* have a little change in his pocket to play poker. That's a *real* gambler. I've seen them before. It's like a drunk finding himself on Sunday without a dime for beer. It doesn't make any difference what he's got in the bank. He wants the beer *then*. Mr. Fox wanted to win back what he lost. He didn't, I'm sorry to say—and he lost everything else.

"As for *your* losings, you can stop the 'retainer' checks you gave me yesterday, if you haven't thought of that already. But I'm going to keep the IOU's just in case either one of you gets rich." They heard a door open in the other room. "Of course you'll both welsh, but I can cause a little trouble." He turned to greet *Maresciallo* Rizzi.

CHAPTER TWENTY-TWO

Maresciallo Rizzi was flanked by two *carabinieri* who regarded him as two inferiors must regard a superior if they also, one day, will become superiors. The *Maresciallo* was beaming at William.

"At least we don't have another murder on our hands. A suicide means a lot of paper work but most of it is standardized. I can get someone else to do it." He looked pointedly at one of his men.

"Massimo was telling the truth, then?"

"Yes—the lawyer is already making the funeral arrangements."

William looked at Sims and Voltor. "I was explaining what happened, *Maresciallo*. As you know, these two gentlemen are involved."

Rizzi grimmaced. His assistants listened intently, bent on improving their secondary school English. "Very much involved, according to them. Isn't that so, Mr. Voltor? Mr. Sims?" He bowed slightly to each one.

Henry had turned angrily to the window. Anson folded his arms and scowled.

Rizzi nodded to William. "The interesting thing about this case is that everyone has told me that the old woman was murdered except the murderer and the one person who had proof—Miss Johns. Two of you had something to gain by informing and I would probably have dropped the case if it hadn't been for you, young man. When you came to me and said you suspected that Mrs. Sheridan had been murdered I decided to investigate. I could see no reason why you should be telling me this unless you believed it to be the truth. *You* had nothing to gain."

"Nothing but my neck."

"Perhaps you are right. I might have taken you for an accomplice."

William spoke to the old men. "I wasn't sure that Fox had murdered Mrs. Sheridan until yesterday evening when Miss Johns told me about the change which had been taken from the old lady's purse. I had been winning only new coins from him since Saturday. The trouble was that she thought *I* was the killer and she was determined to protect him from me. I knew that the minute she told him about the missing silver her own life was in danger. On the other hand I couldn't prove my own suspicions, so to avoid trouble I locked her in her room."

The *Maresciallo* motioned to one of his assistants, who brought him a chair. He accepted a cigarette and a light from the other. "It is astonishing, young man, how little you know about this particular young woman. If I were twenty years . . ." He sighed and brushed a speck from one of his suede shoes. "A young girl who lies to the police for you because she thinks you are guilty of murder and then openly accuses you of having committed the crime and swears to protect your next victim will never stay prudently behind a locked door. Too much is at stake, you see. She might even think she was doing it for your own good, and beware of ladies of all ages who do things for your own good." He looked up at the assistant on his right, who nodded obediently.

"By the time you called last night," Rizzi continued,

"I was already convinced that Fox had killed the old woman. We had discovered that the barbiturate in her stomach did not match the label of the bottle. When we began to check on Cecil Fox we found that he had been living on credit for the last eighteen months. As he has been a resident of this city—on a lavish scale—for many years, no one complained. But recently his credit has been running thin and there were reports of furniture and other goods being shipped out of the house—presumably sold.

"Mr. Fieramosca had indicated the old man's motive for murdering Mrs. Sheridan and that seemed to fit with the facts. Then, last night, I received a notice of his call. Unfortunately not until well after midnight, as I had taken my children to see one of those peculiar films about the American far west. When I arrived at this house I saw the butler leaving. I thought nothing of it until it was too late. I sent a man upstairs to Mr. Fox's room, but it was jammed shut from the inside. I hurried up and we broke in as quickly as possible. He was dead. Sleeping capsules again, undoubtedly. There was no note or any other sign to indicate suicide, except that victims of violence seldom die smiling. Miss Johns *had* been here. We found her handkerchief lying under this chair. We realized then that she had used the dumb-waiter to get up. She told him about the coins. Why Mr. Fox didn't kill her I don't know, unless he had already guessed that we suspected him.

"One peculiar aspect of the death is that all the clocks in the house have been deliberately broken. Not one of them will operate and the enamel clock on the mantel is completely wrecked, together with an hourglass which doesn't seem to have any sand. Even a sundial in the garden has been destroyed. We believe the old man broke them before he killed himself. When Massimo returned several hours later we tried to question him but he would only say that Mr. Fox had told him he was going to die and that he had sent him with a note to his lawyer. I have just been to see the lawyer and he confirms this. I believe Massimo brought him money, but he will not say how much it was or what it will be used for."

Voltor looked haggard. "It's all gone—the money?"

The *Maresciallo* nodded. "*All* gone. We can't find ten lire in the house. I understand that you 'lent' the old man some. It is too bad you have no record. If you had, I might . . ." He raised his hands in a gesture of futility.

"But he stole it. You *know* he stole it!" Anson cried.

"And the gold. He took that, too." Henry stared bitterly out the window.

"Gold?"

"It was in the hourglass—instead of sand."

Maresciallo Rizzi shrugged. It was a gesture far older than the ancient city around them.

Anson Sims stood in the center of the room and raised his finger heavenward. " 'We brought nothing into this world and it is certain we can carry nothing out of it.' First, Timothy, six, seven!"

William walked into the bedroom. On one side of the bed stood the bottle of Old Dan'l. Lying on the table beside the dumb-waiter was a thumbed copy of *Il Falco degli Spazi*. "I wouldn't be so sure *he* can't," he said, staring at the cupid-faced corpse.

CHAPTER TWENTY-THREE

Celia lay in her bed. It was nearly noon but she had no desire to get up. She didn't feel ill, nor even too much upset by what had happened, but she had so many things to decide for herself that she did not have time yet for other people.

First, she had to decide about William. He was so different from what she had imagined that she was bewildered, and even a little disappointed. And yet she had never so distinctly felt an evil force in a person. Even this morning, as he was telling her all that had happened to poor Mr. Fox, she felt it. Behind his pleasant manner there was something else, something ugly and threatening. A formless danger. What was worse it was directed at her. She *knew* it, without being sure any more that her instincts should be trusted.

There was a knock. She got up and saw two letters being slipped under the door. The maid said something in Italian and Celia called out a faint, "*Grazie.*" She gathered up the letters and hurried back to bed. Outside her window she heard a dog barking. Then there was a splash and silence. She looked at the letters.

One was addressed to her in her own hand. It was like picking up a mirror. It was the letter she had written and mailed on Saturday morning. She opened it and read a few lines. She had written letters to herself since childhood; at first because she was lonely, later from habit. She kept them now in a candy box as a diary. Reading this letter she was shocked to see that her description of the old lady's death was no more moving than the letter she had written on their arrival at Dover.

She dropped it on the bed and picked up the other. It was written in a neat, confident hand on heavy cream stationery. At the bottom of the envelope she read, "*Espresso.*" Celia opened it slowly. She had seen this stationery once before.

Fellow member . . .
When you get this I'll be as dead as last night's beer. I would advise you not to worry about that, because if I were not dead right now you would be. So would your nosy boyfriend. If I could have thought of a way to knock you both off last night without getting caught I would certainly have tried it. But the more I thought about it the more I realized that it had gone too far. I wouldn't have minded killing you, sweet, but if they'd grabbed me too that would have been a waste. Especially as you're a fellow member. One of us has to stay alive to train these brutes. So you're kicking and I'm not and I suppose that's reasonable enough.

To tell you the truth, I don't mind death so much. There has to be a stop somewhere and I started stopping years ago. Your life gets to be a constant bargain which you strike with death. You try to post ransom by killing yourself off slowly. That's all right, but you should be careful not to overpay. Death isn't as strong as all that, at least not in the beginning. Later on, of course, you get weaker. Then it comes, whether you pop off or not. It just comes. So here I am, honey, and you're headed my way.

Do you remember in the garden, when I gave you the sapphire? There used to be twelve of them. When I had the sundial built I promised myself I would give those stones only to women who were worth them. I decided I wouldn't meet more than a dozen of those *before I was too old for it to do me any good. Most pretty girls are like wet stones you find on the beach. You take them home and dry them out and you've got gravel. So you're the last, dolly . . . the last of my dozen hours. After that there isn't much point in going on. Suppose I had met another girl in a month? I didn't mind letting you go without laying a finger on you, honey, but I would hate to have to let you go because* I *wasn't interested.*

I have sent some money to my lawyer for my funeral and to pay up my local debts, even Willy's salary—minus what he has stolen from me with his lousy cards. I hope you will have time and patience to stay in the city and see it . . . I mean the funeral. It is going to be very grand. All the gondolas in Venice will be mine for one day, filled with flowers. Then my coffin will be carried into the bay and dropped in the water while twenty boat-loads of lovely girls gather in a ring around the spot and throw flowers and pretend to cry. It will be tremendously touching. If you want, you can have a boat all to yourself. Just go to my lawyer and he will arrange it. He's also got your fare back. You might pretend to cry. I expect my coffin to be dropped in very deep water. It will fall rapidly, as I shall be specially weighted. Thanks to one of my guests I have in my possession several pounds of gold, all of which I mean to keep. When I finish this letter I will take a great number of sleeping pills and proceed to eat my gold. If I can eat it in chocolates I can eat it straight. I would like you to think of me as a laden galley, come to rest on the floor of a world which celebrates the past. My life has been a relic, my death can be one too.

Yours very truly,
Cecil Fox
(and Mr. Moley)

She leaned back on her pillow. Far above, the mirrors caught her reflection. Poor old man. Poor . . .

But her mind drifted on. She was thinking of William. *Why* was she afraid. Why? She heard the dog bark again and got up. Walking across the room she caught a glimpse of the shepherdess leading the satyr across the front of the commode. She noticed that the girl was smiling—enjoying it. Then why run? Celia threw open the shutters. As she caught sight of the colored roofs she answered her own question. "Of course, silly, to be caught."

She looked down at the water. Some boys were tempting a dog to jump off the side of a barge for pieces of bread. He went willingly. It was not a cruel game. And yet it was difficult, even dangerous, for the dog had to swim a long way before it could get a foothold on the bank and run back to the barge.

Suddenly Celia smiled. She understood. William was dangerous, he was threatening—perhaps he was also evil—just as life was all these things. She had grown up to know death, and to know how not to be afraid of it. But life was something new. It was all a mystery to her, and would be until she learned it. William was offering her the key to that mystery.

She turned and went to the wardrobe. For the first time in her life she was going to dress with the conscious purpose of snaring a man. . . . A not altogether trustworthy, often dangerous and always threatening man. The two letters lay on her bed. Two messages from Death. She would never receive such messages again; at least not while she stayed in the large, sunny, perilous world of the living. On the canal the dog barked and plunged into the water. . . .

THE PERENNIAL LIBRARY MYSTERY SERIES

E. C. Bentley

TRENT'S LAST CASE

"One of the three best detective stories ever written."

—Agatha Christie

TRENT'S OWN CASE

"I won't waste time saying that the plot is sound and the detection satisfying. Trent has not altered a scrap and reappears with all his old humor and charm." —Dorothy L. Sayers

Gavin Black

A DRAGON FOR CHRISTMAS

"Potent excitement!" —*New York Herald Tribune*

THE EYES AROUND ME

"I stayed up until all hours last night reading *The Eyes Around Me*, which is something I do not do very often, but I was so intrigued by the ingeniousness of Mr. Black's plotting and the witty way in which he spins his mystery. I can only say that I enjoyed the book enormously."

—F. van Wyck Mason

YOU WANT TO DIE, JOHNNY?

"Gavin Black doesn't just develop a pressure plot in suspense, he adds uninfected wit, character, charm, and sharp knowledge of the Far East to make rereading as keen as the first race-through." —*Book Week*

Nicholas Blake

THE BEAST MUST DIE

"It remains one more proof that in the hands of a really first-class writer the detective novel can safely challenge comparison with any other variety of fiction." —*The Manchester Guardian*

THE CORPSE IN THE SNOWMAN

"If there is a distinction between the novel and the detective story (which we do not admit), then this book deserves a high place in both categories." —*The New York Times*

THE DREADFUL HOLLOW

"Pace unhurried, characters excellent, reasoning solid."

—*San Francisco Chronicle*

END OF CHAPTER
". . . admirably solid . . . an adroit formal detective puzzle backed up by firm characterization and a knowing picture of London publishing."
—*The New York Times*

HEAD OF A TRAVELER
"Another grade A detective story of the right old jigsaw persuasion."
—*New York Herald Tribune Book Review*

MINUTE FOR MURDER
"An outstanding mystery novel. Mr. Blake's writing is a delight in itself."
—*The New York Times*

THE MORNING AFTER DEATH
"One of Blake's best."
—Rex Warner

A PENKNIFE IN MY HEART
"Style brilliant . . . and suspenseful."
—*San Francisco Chronicle*

THE PRIVATE WOUND
[Blake's] best novel in a dozen years . . . . An intensely penetrating study of sexual passion . . . . A powerful story of murder and its aftermath."
—Anthony Boucher, *The New York Times*

A QUESTION OF PROOF
"The characters in this story are unusually well drawn, and the suspense is well sustained."
—*The New York Times*

THE SAD VARIETY
"It is a stunner. I read it instead of eating, instead of sleeping."
—Dorothy Salisbury Davis

THE SMILER WITH THE KNIFE
"An extraordinarily well written and entertaining thriller."
—*Saturday Review of Literature*

THOU SHELL OF DEATH
"It has all the virtues of culture, intelligence and sensibility that the most exacting connoisseur could ask of detective fiction."
—*The Times* [London] *Literary Supplement*

THE WHISPER IN THE GLOOM
"One of the most entertaining suspense-pursuit novels in many seasons."
—*The New York Times*

Nicolas Blake (cont'd)

THE WIDOW'S CRUISE
"A stirring suspense. . . . The thrilling tale leaves nothing to be desired."
—*Springfield Republican*

THE WORM OF DEATH
"It [The Worm of Death] is one of Blake's very best—and his best is better than almost anyone's." —Louis Untermeyer

George Harmon Coxe

MURDER WITH PICTURES
"[Coxe] has hit the bull's-eye with his first shot."
—*The New York Times*

Edmund Crispin

BURIED FOR PLEASURE
"Absolute and unalloyed delight."
—Anthony Boucher, *The New York Times*

Kenneth Fearing

THE BIG CLOCK
"It will be some time before chill-hungry clients meet again so rare a compound of irony, satire, and icy-fingered narrative. *The Big Clock* is . . . a psychothriller you won't put down." —*Weekly Book Review*

Andrew Garve

THE ASHES OF LODA
"Garve . . . embellishes a fine fast adventure story with a more credible picture of the U.S.S.R. than is offered in most thrillers."
—*The New York Times Book Review*

THE CUCKOO LINE AFFAIR
". . . an agreeable and ingenious piece of work." —*The New Yorker*

A HERO FOR LEANDA
"One can trust Mr. Garve to put a fresh twist to any situation, and the ending is really a lovely surprise." —*The Manchester Guardian*

MURDER THROUGH THE LOOKING GLASS
". . . refreshingly out-of-the-way and enjoyable . . . highly recommended to all comers." —*Saturday Review*

NO TEARS FOR HILDA
"It starts fine and finishes finer. I got behind on breathing watching Max get not only his man but his woman, too." —Rex Stout

THE RIDDLE OF SAMSON
"The story is an excellent one, the people are quite likable, and the writing is superior." —*Springfield Republican*

Michael Gilbert

BLOOD AND JUDGMENT
"Gilbert readers need scarcely be told that the characters all come alive at first sight, and that his surpassing talent for narration enhances any plot. . . . Don't miss." —*San Francisco Chronicle*

THE BODY OF A GIRL
"Does what a good mystery should do: open up into all kinds of ramifications, with untold menace behind the action. At the end, there is a bang-up climax, and it is a pleasure to see how skilfully Gilbert wraps everything up." —*The New York Times Book Review*

THE DANGER WITHIN
"Michael Gilbert has nicely combined some elements of the straight detective story with plenty of action, suspense, and adventure, to produce a superior thriller." —*Saturday Review*

DEATH HAS DEEP ROOTS
"Trial scenes superb; prowl along Loire vivid chase stuff; funny in right places; a fine performance throughout." —*Saturday Review*

FEAR TO TREAD
"Merits serious consideration as a work of art." —*The New York Times*

C. W. Grafton

BEYOND A REASONABLE DOUBT
"A very ingenious tale of murder . . . a brilliant and gripping narrative." —Jacques Barzun and Wendell Hertig Taylor

Edward Grierson

THE SECOND MAN
"One of the best trial-testimony books to have come along in quite a while." —*The New Yorker*

Cyril Hare

AN ENGLISH MURDER
"By a long shot, the best crime story I have read for a long time. Everything is traditional, but originality does not suffer. The setting is perfect. Full marks to Mr. Hare." —*Irish Press*

TRAGEDY AT LAW
"An extremely urbane and well-written detective story."
—*The New York Times*

UNTIMELY DEATH
"The English detective story at its quiet best, meticulously underplayed, rich in perceivings of the droll human animal and ready at the last with a neat surprise which has been there all the while had we but wits to see it." —*New York Herald Tribune Book Review*

WHEN THE WIND BLOWS
"The best, unquestionably, of all the Hare stories, and a masterpiece by any standards."
—Jacques Barzun and Wendell Hertig Taylor, *A Catalogue of Crime*

WITH A BARE BODKIN
"One of the best detective stories published for a long time."
—*The Spectator*

Matthew Head

THE CABINDA AFFAIR (*available 6/81*)
"An absorbing whodunit and a distinguished novel of atmosphere."
—Anthony Boucher, *The New York Times*

MURDER AT THE FLEA CLUB (*available 6/81*)
"The true delight is in Head's style, its limpid ease combined with humor and an awesome precision of phrase." —*San Francisco Chronicle*

M. V. Heberden

ENGAGED TO MURDER
"Smooth plotting." —*The New York Times*

James Hilton

WAS IT MURDER?
"The story is well planned and well written."
—*The New York Times*

Elspeth Huxley

THE AFRICAN POISON MURDERS (*available 5/81*)
"Obscure venom, manical mutilations, deadly bush fire, thrilling climax compose major opus.... Top-flight."
—*Saturday Review of Literature*

Francis Iles

BEFORE THE FACT
"Not many 'serious' novelists have produced character studies to compare with Iles's internally terrifying portrait of the murderer in *Before the Fact,* his masterpiece and a work truly deserving the appellation of unique and beyond price." —Howard Haycraft

MALICE AFORETHOUGHT
"It is a long time since I have read anything so good as *Malice Aforethought,* with its cynical humour, acute criminology, plausible detail and rapid movement. It makes you hug yourself with pleasure."
—H. C. Harwood, *Saturday Review*

Lange Lewis

THE BIRTHDAY MURDER
"Almost perfect in its playlike purity and delightful prose."
—Jacques Barzun and Wendell Hertig Taylor

Arthur Maling

LUCKY DEVIL
"The plot unravels at a fast clip, the writing is breezy and Maling's approach is as fresh as today's stockmarket quotes."
—*Louisville Courier Journal*

RIPOFF
"A swiftly paced story of today's big business is larded with intrigue as a Ralph Nader-type investigates an insurance scandal and is soon on the run from a hired gun and his brother. . . . Engrossing and credible."
—*Booklist*

SCHROEDER'S GAME
"As the title indicates, this Schroeder is up to something, and the unravelling of his game is a diverting and sufficiently blood-soaked entertainment." —*The New Yorker*

Thomas Sterling

THE EVIL OF THE DAY
"Prose as witty and subtle as it is sharp and clear. . .characters unconventionally conceived and richly bodied forth . . . . In short, a novel to be treasured." —Anthony Boucher, *The New York Times*

Julian Symons

THE BELTING INHERITANCE
"A superb whodunit in the best tradition of the detective story."
—August Derleth, *Madison Capital Times*

BLAND BEGINNING
"Mr. Symons displays a deft storytelling skill, a quiet and literate wit, a nice feeling for character, and detectival ingenuity of a high order."
—Anthony Boucher, *The New York Times*

BOGUE'S FORTUNE
"There's a touch of the old sardonic humour, and more than a touch of style." —*The Spectator*

THE BROKEN PENNY
"The most exciting, astonishing and believable spy story to appear in years. —Anthony Boucher, *The New York Times Book Review*

THE COLOR OF MURDER
"A singularly unostentatious and memorably brilliant detective story."
—*New York Herald Tribune Book Review*

THE 31ST OF FEBRUARY
"Nobody has painted a more gruesome picture of the advertising business since Dorothy Sayers wrote 'Murder Must Advertise', and very few people have written a more entertaining or dramatic mystery story."
—*The New Yorker*

Dorothy Stockbridge Tillet
(John Stephen Strange)

THE MAN WHO KILLED FORTESCUE
"Better than average." —*Saturday Review of Literature*

Henry Kitchell Webster

WHO IS THE NEXT? (*available 5/81*)
"A double murder, private-plane piloting, a neat impersonation, and a delicate courtship are adroitly combined by a writer who knows how to use the language." —Jacques Barzun and Wendell Hertig Taylor